Shadows In the Flames

Shadows, Volume 2

Scott G. Gibson

Published by Scott Gibson, 2020.

This is a work of fiction. Similarities to real people, places, or events are entirely coincidental.

SHADOWS IN THE FLAMES

First edition. November 13, 2020.

Copyright © 2020 Scott G. Gibson.

Written by Scott G. Gibson.

Also by Scott G. Gibson

Bad Luck Bevin
Bad Luck Bevin

Shadows
Shadows of a Nightmare
Shadows In the Flames

Standalone
Place Your Hand in Mine
Making Tracks

Watch for more at https://scottggibson.wordpress.com/.

To Jess, Liesel and Jonathan, who light the way through
the darkness

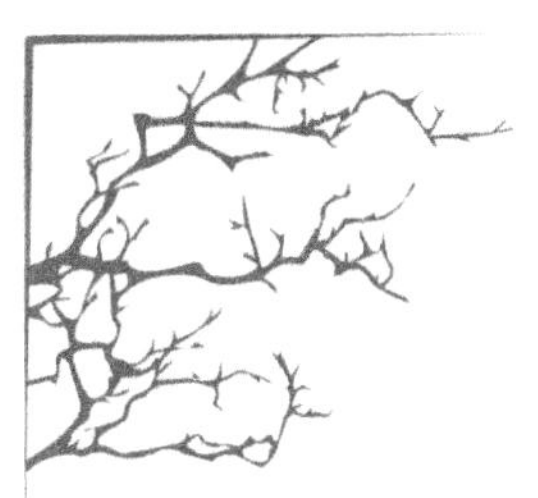

Foreword

"For the world is changing: I feel it in the water, I feel it in the earth, and I smell it in the air." – J.R.R. Tolkien.

Every day, our world seems to teeter on the edge of chaos. Although we may not realise it as we go about our everyday business, if we were to view the world's history, we would see a series of events that are both linked and completely random.

Our technologies bring us closer on a communication level, yet drag us further away from a compassionate, empathetic standpoint. Disagreements become hate-filled personal attacks on social media. News channels stream doom and gloom, avoiding the happier news to promote a daily vibe of misery.

But don't lose hope! While there are those whose voices yell louder than others, filling the daily void with hatred and vitriol, our world is full of wonderful people, sharing love and optimism. There are so many people whose acts of love and care go unnoticed, but continue nonetheless, showing integrity we wish all our leaders valued.

We experienced many of these beautiful souls while in hospital with our son, Jonathan.

While fiction may sometimes bring dystopian futures to the forefront of our brains, it stands as a voice of warning. An alarm of things we must remember, as these trolls work to divide and conquer. Authors throughout history have (sometimes correctly) predicted the future, others have taught us valuable lessons to prevent the apocalypse.

Speculative fiction allows us to ask questions about the world—safely in our imaginations—while we consider that some things in life aren't as bad as they could be.

Two stories within this anthology (*Atheria* and *Armalina*) are prequel tales to a series of young adult fantasy novels I am currently working on, and look forward to sharing with you in the near future. Other stories were a mix of either my predictions for the future, or trying to escape my present reality.

So sit back, get comfortable, and enjoy the following stories. May they terrorise you and help you realise that the real world isn't as bad as it could be.

Not yet anyway.

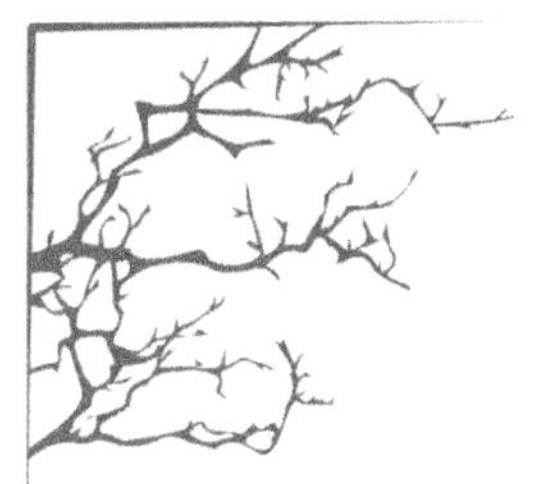

Atheria

The sky was ablaze. Streaks of orange rained down towards Arthur as he looked up into the night, eyes bleary from his stolen slumber. The stars seemed to fall earthwards, released from their anchors.

Arthur's goats bleated noisily, their white fur glistening in the orange glow. His dad had sent him out with the herd to graze the pastures near their shack, and Arthur had jumped at the chance. Sleeping under the stars was much better than being near his dad when he had been drinking. Arthur had been surprised at the order; he had once lost ten goats from the herd—a huge loss to his father's wealth—and his father had been furious. Arthur could still feel the wounds from the thrashing he had received.

The goats needed fattening up in preparation for market, and his father had just bartered a fresh barrel of ale. *He'll be hopeless for a few days*, Arthur thought.

The sky was filled with a spider web of flames and, as he looked on, Arthur heard a rumbling sound, getting louder with each passing second. His heart quickened its pace as he looked around at the frightened herd of goats. Arthur tried uselessly to count the goats, but they were moving around too much in the dancing orange light.

There was an explosion of fire and dirt about one hundred metres from Arthur, sending the goats fleeing, some in the direction of his home, others going the opposite way. *Father is going to be livid,* Arthur thought, *especially if I'm unable to find them all.* He felt the sense of duty to go running after them, to ensure the safety of his herd. But an overwhelming curiosity drew him towards the crash site, where smoke glowed orange in the eerie light. As he walked towards the impact zone, a burning smell invaded his nose and he picked up his pace.

Curiosity smouldered within Arthur like the sky around him. He started running. The singed grass grew closer, the ground glowing amber. As he approached, Arthur could see a stone nestled in the middle of a crater about twice as deep as he was tall. The rock was about his height, only wider and more rotund, and Arthur examined it with growing interest. He could feel the warmth emanating from the area, washing over him, reminding him of the cooking fire he often worked with back home. The night had been cool, but now Arthur began to sweat as he scrambled down the declivity to the rock. Cold rivulets trickled down his face, soaking into his clothes. He could smell the damp soil as it slid down, loosened by his descent.

In the sky, the orange transitioned back to black, the bright stars shining through now that the rocks had stopped plummeting to the ground.

Arthur returned his gaze to the rock, staring intently as the orange glow faded slowly. As the rock darkened, a symbol was revealed, glowing brightly. A triangle the size of Arthur's hand surrounded a curved line, like the blade of a scythe.

The sweat on Arthur's body began to cool as Emilica's winds picked up, bathing him in icy air. His body was chilled to the bones, his old, well-worn clothes no barrier to the climate. He pulled his water pouch from his threadbare pocket and trickled some onto the rock, where it sizzled and steamed.

A loud crack resonated through the air and, as Arthur watched, the rock began to split. Arthur moved back quickly, feeling his back hit the edge of the crater, unsure what to expect from the alien rock before him. He put the pouch back into his pocket, as if hiding it would reverse the damage he had caused.

Morning was on its way, the sun preparing to warm the air and chase away the shadows of night. The horizon showed faint colouring, unnoticed by Arthur as he stared at the cracking stone. The split in the stone widened, and Arthur could see leather pushing its way out. As more of the thick skin protruded from the rock, Arthur began to see bones stretching the leather, and razor-sharp claws the size of his fingers.

It's a wing! Arthur thought, his curiosity fully piqued. He took a step forward, his trembling hand stretched out as if it had a mind of its own. The wing looked like the kites he helped fly on winter solstice day, when the village's farmers prayed for spring and bountiful harvests. *It must be some kind of egg!*

The egg began to split wider, more of the body emerging behind the wing. Arthur saw more claws, leathery skin, crimson spikes, white teeth, and yellow eyes.

During his youth his father had shared wondrous tales of dragons, before falling asleep, catatonic in his drunken stupor. But they were stories, carried down from father to son for generations. Myths!

They weren't real.

And yet, here in front of him, Arthur saw living proof that they were real. The beast had escaped its egg, little shards of shell—as hard as rock—littered the scorched ground around it. Arthur could feel the heat emanating from the creature as he stared into its yellow eyes, entranced. He felt like the dragon was trying to read him, judge his worth.

Or decide whether to eat him.

The dragon's snout moved towards Arthur, its nostrils flaring as it sniffed, snorting loudly. Arthur saw a black tongue flicking out between its pointed teeth. Arthur felt a quiver of fear, his hand edging closer, wanting only to turn and run. The dragon opened its mouth, now only inches from his hand. Small curls of steam rose from its nostrils.

"Hey there, fella," Arthur said, his voice shaking, mirroring his outstretched hand. "Please don't eat me. I wouldn't make a good meal." The dragon continued staring into his own eyes.

And it nodded, before moving its snout beneath his hand. He rubbed the top of its warm snout, feeling the rough skin beneath his fingers.

Does it understand me? Arthur wondered. The dragon tilted its head away, yellow eyes still locked on Arthur's blue ones. He could feel his dark hair matted to his scalp.

"Can you understand me?" Arthur said, tilting his own head. The dragon nodded, scratching its chest with a sharp claw. With an exertion of mental effort, Arthur drew his gaze away from the dragon's eyes and looked where the beast was scratching. The same symbol from the egg coloured the dragon's dark grey chest. The insignia was a light blue like the morning sky brightening the world around them. Arthur looked back at the dragon's eyes.

"Do you have a name?" Arthur asked. The dragon shook its head before looking down at the ground, as if searching for something. The dragon raked its claw through the debris of its shell, before picking up a shard and passing it to Arthur. Standing tall above

Arthur, the dragon looked down, and Arthur was surprised at its immense bulk, amazed at how it had fit inside the egg. The beast must have been about the size of his one-room shack.

Arthur looked now at what the dragon had passed him. It was part of the shell, with a claw hole drilled in. Flipping it over, Arthur saw the same symbol that adorned the dragon's chest, and recognised it from the egg.

"Am I... Am I supposed to wear this?" he asked, glancing up at the dragon, brows furrowed. The dragon nodded. Arthur felt the warmth of the egg medallion in his hand as he fumbled for his empty coin purse. He hadn't used it for some time and remembered the last time it had held a coin, many moons ago. He had found a copper, and had used it to buy a loaf of bread and a joint of cold mutton for his journey to a pasture far away. Often Arthur had taken his father's bow to hunt, and was skilled at hitting his target, but on some occasions, such as when he had found the coin, his father was sober enough to prevent him taking the valuable weapon, hunger looming in wait.

Arthur removed the leather string he used to tie up the sack and threaded it through the hole in the medallion. When he had tied a few knots, Arthur put the cord around his head, the medallion falling beneath his shirt to rest against the bare skin of his chest. Warmth spread like fire through his torso, making Arthur tense in shock. He had not expected such a quick reaction and, when the warmth reached his head, a peculiar sensation tingled through him. A voice seemed to echo quietly in his brain, becoming louder with each passing moment, until it was as if someone was talking right beside his ear. Except his ear heard nothing.

What is happening? Arthur thought, staring down at the medallion.

"It is our connection," the dragon said, her voice smoother and more melodic than he had anticipated. At least, Arthur thought it was female. Once again, he seemed to hear the voice without any sound travelling through the air.

"You are female, aren't you?" Arthur said.

The dragon chuckled. "Yes, I am what you would call female. The insignia you wear around your neck connects our minds and strengthens our bond. I do not know why, but I was sent to join with you. What is special about you, Mister...?"

"Arthur. My name is Arthur." Technically his full name was Arthur, son of Richard, but with a father like his... "Just Arthur."

"Well, Just Arthur, you can call me... Call me Atheria. I think that seems to suit me since we are bonded, would you agree?"

"It's a brilliant name!" Arthur replied. "But there's nothing brilliant about me. I'm just a goat herder. I'm not really good at anything. I'm not even that great at keeping the goats alive. I, um... I've lost a few before."

"I see. And there is nothing you can do well?" Atheria looked deep into Arthur's eyes, as if invisible hands were rummaging within him.

"Well, I can shoot a bow pretty good. I usually hit my target. Not perfect, mind you. But enough to stay fed. And I guess I've learned to hide, and live with pain, so that's a plus." And he had. Arthur had certainly survived many beatings from his father, and as a result, had learned to hide relatively well from his father, and the prey he was hunting. "I don't suppose you know where you've come from, or why?"

"No, but I have picked up a lot of what you know. I guess our first action will be to search for the other dragons who fell. Based on what you saw, some of them are close by over towards that forest there." Atheria pointed a claw to the west, and Arthur followed her gaze, seeing only the tips of the trees beyond the crater.

Arthur looked back at the dragon, his eyes roaming over her wings. "Can you fly, Atheria?" She looked down at Arthur and flapped her wings slowly, as if remembering their existence.

"I am yet to try," Atheria replied, flapping her wings more quickly. Arthur felt the wind pushing over him, stirring the dirt around them, but Atheria's feet lifted only a finger's gap from the ground. Her wings slowed down to stop on her back. "I am too weak to fly yet; I need food."

"Are you strong enough to walk? I'll be able to find something for you to eat, even if it is some of the goats I'm supposed to keep safe. If only I had my bow, I could hunt some other animals for you." Arthur's stomach began to rumble as he realised he had not eaten breakfast, and had not brought enough food to provide even a mouthful.

"I am strong enough to walk for some distance, thanks," Atheria said. "Let us get going." Arthur watched as Atheria began to scramble up the slope, her four strong legs tensing as she hooked her claws into the dirt, her wings flapping softly to help her climb. Her tail moved back and forth, providing balance.

When she reached the top, Atheria looked back down at Arthur, who still stood gaping up at the dragon. "Please tell me you are coming, Arthur. I am famished!"

Arthur scrambled up after her, using the holes from her claws as foot holds. Finally, with sweat soaking his body, pouring down his face, he reached the top, breathing in the fresh scent of the morning air. He sighed as the breeze washed over his face, ruffled his hair. They began to walk towards the forest.

To the west of the pasture, in front of where they walked, was a small forest of oak, maple, and beech, stripped of all but a few brittle leaves, backed by the dark winter richness of assorted spruce and pine. The ground, where the sun only just managed to poke its dusty fingers, was covered with fallen damp leaves and pine needles which would soften the sound of their footsteps to a soft crunch. A shallow creek trickled along the edge of the forest, creating a musical burble to anyone within earshot. Arthur used it regularly as a source for water.

They began heading for the path through the woods, the sun shining on their backs, casting long shadows on the grass in front of them.

"It was quite a show, your entry. Freaked the goats out," Arthur said, trying unsuccessfully to cover the rumbling of his stomach with his voice.

"Yes, I can imagine it would have been quite spectacular, yet ever so daunting." Atheria stumbled forwards beside Arthur, her claws almost dragging along the ground. They approached the creek and Arthur rushed to quench his thirst, having used the last of his supply on the hot, unhatched egg. His fingers almost froze as he scooped it into his parched mouth, before refilling his pouch. With a gasp, he caught his breath and relished the coolness spreading through his mouth and down to his stomach. Atheria knelt beside him to drink, steam rising as her mouth touched the water's surface.

When Arthur had satisfied his thirst, he stood up and rubbed his hands together, trying to remove the icy shards within his bloodstream. He wondered if Atheria could feel the cold as savagely as he could. It seemed like snow had started falling inside his stomach, and slowly, when he had moved closer to Atheria's eternal warmth, he started to warm up again.

"Yes, Arthur, I do feel the cold," Atheria said, "but it is less severe than you, though perhaps, more of a shock." Arthur grinned bashfully at her. A loud rumble reverberated through Atheria's stomach. "I must find food soon," she said. "I can smell fresh meat further ahead through the woods."

With that, Atheria began moving quickly, her large legs pounding the ground, her mind focussed on the hunt. Arthur could feel the vibrations run through his legs as he walked. He wondered if trees could feel like he did, perhaps worried they might topple with enough vibrating force.

Arthur couldn't tell how long they had been traipsing through the forest, but his legs were sore from moving so quickly to keep up with Atheria, who was continuing to expand the vast distance between them. The sound of bleating wafted towards them, and Arthur noticed Atheria put on a burst of speed. Looking up, Arthur saw some of his escaped goats attempting to outrun the giant lizard behind them.

They were unsuccessful in their attempt.

Atheria's jaw was big enough to swallow each goat whole, making Arthur wonder when they died. He hoped it had been quick and they weren't left to suffer, stewing painfully inside her immense stomach, their bleats dying slowly with them.

Arthur cringed at the thought of his father's reaction when he noticed the goats missing.

Once Atheria had devoured each of the goats that had wandered through the forest, they continued walking, hoping to discover the crash zone of other dragon eggs. Ahead of them, Arthur could see a large crater which knocked over trees to make a small clearing. They edged forward, alert to sounds of other dragons nearby. Arthur could smell smoke on the air, the trees smouldering from the heat. He heard nothing but their own footsteps, and the sound of his ragged breathing.

"It has gone," Atheria said, peering down into the ditch. "It has hatched and headed off somewhere. It could be miles away by now."

"Any clues which direction?" Arthur asked, finally catching up to Atheria at the edge of the crater. Arthur could see the shards of rock that once housed the dragon, broken in the singed dirt.

"Could be any. My guess would be in the direction of the nearest town. It is most likely to have food to break its fast." Atheria peered around them, eyes piercing through the forest. "Which way is that?"

"Back the way we came. My father's hut is on the road that heads to the castle. I can lead the way if you like, but it could be a half day's walk." Arthur glanced at Atheria's wings. "Any chance you can fly yet?"

Atheria squatted closer to the ground, preparing her legs to spring upwards. Her wings moved slowly on her back, before she gave an enormous leap, smoke blowing from her nostrils with the effort. She floated a few metres above ground, jiggling up and down, before coming back to rest on the ground.

"I am still too weak," she panted, her head tilted to the ground. Arthur moved over to her, resting his hand on what he thought was her shoulder. Warmth spread through his hands, removing any last trace of the freezing water.

"It's okay. You will get there with some practice and time... Let's head to my father's house and perhaps, when he sees you, he may give you more goats out of fear," Arthur said, hoping to boost her confidence. After all, he had no idea whether dragons actually could fly or not, considering their immense size. All the animals he had seen with wings could fly, but they were significantly smaller than Atheria.

"I sense some confusion in you. I understand, Arthur, and I do not blame you. I will keep trying," Atheria said. "Let us do as you suggest, and perhaps we will have some success."

They began walking back the way they had come, following the same track. This time, Atheria walked more slowly, allowing Arthur to keep stride beside her. Both were silent, allowing Arthur to listen to the sounds of the forest around him, as he usually would whenever he was by himself. He had spent many days and nights exploring the land around him, hunting, ensuring he kept well clear of the king's deer.

There was no way venison could taste good enough to risk death.

"I sense a history in these parts for you. It must have some kind of connection, some feeling of family. Am I correct?" Atheria said, her head tilted towards Arthur, allowing her eyes to bore deep within him.

"My father hasn't really been the loving type. Well, not to me, at least. Maybe he was to my mother. I've realised that *something* must have attracted her to him. I never knew her, so I will never be able to ask." Arthur's mind delved deep within his memory, shutting out the details around them as they walked.

"Since I can remember, I've explored these parts, mostly while my father is out cold. It's always felt like home. Something about its predictability, and reliability resonates with me, you know? Like, you light a fire and you know it'll burn until the wood is burnt out. You know the trees will always stand in the one spot, and sway in the breeze. The animals will run or hide from me, unless I hide well. But humans..." Arthur paused, choking back tears. "Humans are unpredictable. They change their mind as the breeze blows in a storm. Possibly just as destructive. People want power, control; no matter over what. They'll have it, and there's just no way of knowing what they're thinking, or what they'll do next."

Arthur fell silent once more. They came to the edge of the forest, the sound of babbling water growing louder. The sun had risen high in the sky, casting short shadows over the swaying grass beneath them.

Atheria stopped, her body rigid. "I smell another human ahead," she said, stepping back into the trees. Arthur squinted into the distance, seeing what appeared to be a man pulling a wagon heading in their direction. Arthur peered back, checking to ensure Atheria was as well-hidden as possible. He could see her dark mass hunched down through the trees. Taking a few sips from his water pouch, he waited for the traveller, refilling it from the stream for something to do.

The traveller moved slowly, bent forward against the weight of the wagon, shoulders hunched. Arthur sensed that there was an immense determination, despite the appearance of resignation. If the traveller had seen Arthur, who was now sitting in the grass by the stream, he gave no sign, continuing to move forward at the same speed, one foot plodding in front of the other.

Finally, the traveller had moved to within calling distance, still unaware of Arthur's—or Atheria's—presence.

"What news from Emilica?" Arthur called out, trying hard to smile warmly. The traveller stopped, looking up, his eyebrows arched to the sky, face framed by his travelling hood. His mouth hung open, revealing yellow teeth.

"'Oo are you?" the traveller asked suspiciously, dropping the handles of his wagon. "I be but a travelling peasant. I mean you no 'arm."

"I am Arthur, son of Richard. I live a short distance yonder," Arthur said, pointing. "I live with my father."

"Your father the goat 'erder? Yes, I saw your father. 'E looked mad, 'e did! Mutterin' somethin' 'bout missin' goats, or some such. Familiar, 'e was, but 'e was too drunk to know my face. Been many a year since I saw 'im. Anyway, I told 'im, I said, squire, I said, there be dragons in the kingdom; on their way to the castle, they be 'eadin'. Big, lizard-worms, breathin' fire and the like. I just come from there, runnin' for me life. When I left, even the king's guards were runnin' round like a chicken with its 'ead cut off." The traveller began cackling, high pitched and unnatural.

"What's your name?" Arthur asked, trying to bring back some level of humanity to the man.

"My name? I go by many names." More cackles.

"What shall I call you?" Arthur's teeth were clenched, trying to keep the frustration out of his tone.

"Call me what you like; just don't call me late for dinner." More manic laughter made Arthur groan, his shoulders slumped. *I'm getting nowhere with this man*, he thought.

"Did you see anything fall from yonder whence you came?" Arthur tried again.

"I was a soldier once; I saw many things fall, I did. Yes. Many men fell, too. Men who fought beside me. Your father was one of them, though he lived, if my mind tells words of truth." The traveller was nonsensical. His father hadn't been a warrior. *Had he?*

"How many of these dragons did you see?" Arthur asked.

"Now there's a question I can answer. Four. No, five dragons. Or was it four?" He counted his fingers. "Per'aps it *was* only four." Arthur glanced back where Atheria had hidden, thinking about the missing dragon from the crater. How many goats had he already lost to the other dragons?

"Someone needs to fight those there dragons, young'un. Not me; I did my fightin' in the name of the king. If you be 'eadin' that way, best pack a weapon. Swords won't make the cut, but arrows will hit the mark. Keep it in mind, young'un." The traveller picked up his wagon handles, hunched forward and began walking. As he trudged past Arthur, he smiled, his lips baring back over his teeth, revealing a few missing at the back.

Arthur turned and watched him go, shaking his head in disbelief. With a furtive glance to Atheria's hiding place, he saw she would be out of sight from the traveller as he passed her.

Once he had disappeared through the trees, Atheria crawled out, sniffing the air. She moved over to Arthur, wisps of smoke trailing from her nostrils.

"I can feel my throat warming up. I believe it is a good sign," Atheria said as she approached Arthur. "As we walk, I will move my wings and stretch them out. Those goats made me feel stronger. Come, let us have one last drink and move on."

Arthur watched as Atheria guzzled down more water, steam rising around her head once again, giving her a mystic appearance. Tendrils of vapour twirled among Atheria's spikes, climbing up and around her body.

When her thirst was satiated, they moved on into the early afternoon sun, moving as quickly as Arthur's human legs would allow. They were both eager to continue their quest. They hadn't spoken about their plans for when they finally met the other dragons, but Arthur hoped they would be friendly. After all, Atheria was of their kind. However, he also knew that humans had been at war for many an age, and they too were of the same species.

Maybe dragons would be more intelligent than humans.

Many times when Arthur had been out with his goats, he had been forced to pry two bucks away from each other, their tiny horns ready for impact. Dragons had a lot more inbuilt weapons with which to attack each other; humans just created more, each more destructive than the last.

"When we get to my father's shack, perhaps it might be best if you wait behind, out of sight," Arthur said tentatively. "I don't know how father will take you."

"If you think it is best, then I will do as you wish. Call my name if you would like me to come," Atheria said, stopping where they were. "I can just make out a shack ahead, and can smell the man who works there. I can hear him muttering something about missing goats. I believe your name has been mentioned a number of times already."

An invisible fist clenched Arthur's heart.

Arthur could see his father's shack looming ahead, growing bigger with each step. A ball of dread grew inside him, making his steps more arduous. His father was outside the shack, chopping wood with his heavy axe. There were a few goats munching on feed in their small pen, bleating softly. Arthur wondered if they knew the fate of their missing herd. As if on cue, their bleats grew louder as Arthur approached.

At the crescendo of sound, Richard stopped chopping and leaned on his axe. "Well, if it isn't the prodigal son himself. Where's my goats? Let me guess, lost them again, no doubt. Loser. Why I ever thought I could trust you with a bunch of living creatures, I don't know." Richard spat each sentence out with distaste, getting louder with each loaded insult. Arthur could see spittle flecking his lips and chin. Aware of his sagging shoulders, Arthur lifted them in an attempt to stand straight and tall.

"They were eaten by dragons, if you must know."

Richard snorted. "Dragons! What a load of pig swill! I was in the king's army for *years* before you were born, and not once did we encounter *dragons*. Enemy soldiers, assassins, usurpers, thieves, braggarts and rapists. But never dragons, boy! You're out of your mind!"

"Had you been awake instead of passed out cold like the pathetic alcoholic you are, you would have seen them falling from the sky. Didn't you stop to wonder why there is smoke over there on the horizon?" Arthur pointed, trying to calm his breathing. His voice getting louder with each uttered word. "You're pathetic!"

"How dare you!" Richard said coldly. "I raised you from a baby after you *murdered* your mother! My wife! And this is how you talk to me?"

Arthur felt guilt claw at his stomach, but remained stoic. Atheria was waiting behind him; dragons were attacking the kingdom. No way would his father continue his aggression with a dragon waiting with open jaws.

Richard raised his axe, holding it in both hands. "Get out! I don't want to see you back here ever again!"

Arthur remained standing where he was, not bothering to listen to his father's shouted directions. He called for Atheria in his mind, letting her presence fill his thoughts. Lifting the axe higher, Richard paced closer towards his son, his teeth clenched.

"I said... get... away... from... here! You... are... no... longer... MY SON!" His arms began to move the axe forward.

And they stopped. Arthur had squinted, waiting for the blow to fall. He felt the ground vibrate softly beneath his feet as Atheria bounded forward, roaring loudly. Then, great gusts of wind threatened to blow Arthur off his feet. Strengthening his stance, he turned to see Atheria's great bulk in the air above, wings flapping powerfully. Overjoyed, he felt his heart rise to meet her. *She could fly!*

Arthur turned back to his father, and saw he had collapsed to the ground, the axe lying beneath his back. Leaning forward, Arthur grabbed the handle, grunting with the exertion of pulling it from beneath his father. There was no way Arthur was leaving the weapon with such a violent man!

"What do we do now, Arthur?" Atheria said from behind him, now with four claws firmly on the ground. "While we stay here, your kingdom burns. That smoke on the horizon is not a cooking fire."

"I know," Arthur said, holding the axe in both hands, "but I'm unprepared. *We* are unprepared." He sighed heavily, shoulders slumped. "I can shoot a quiver of arrows in under a minute, but never surrounded by flames. I can hit the target, but have only ever done so standing firmly on the ground. I can kill a small, furry animal for food, but never tried on a dragon. How will we save the kingdom? What if you are killed by association?"

"So look me over now. Look for the weak spots. Then we will practise. I will practise flying and breathing fire and swooping. You practise shooting, swinging the axe and riding on my back. We must be quick; every moment spent here means more destruction in the kingdom." Atheria moved over to the remaining goats in the pen, paused momentarily, before swallowing each one whole.

"Sorry, Arthur. I needed the energy, and thought perhaps you would not mind, considering what lies ahead of us."

Arthur glanced at his father, passed out on the ground. "Not at all. I've always wanted to do something other than being the lonely goat herder. You've done me a favour." He could feel Atheria smiling back at him as she took off into the air, flying high and twirling around, somersaulting, testing her skills. Nothing was more awesome to Arthur than watching her flying, enjoying her newfound freedom. Sensing her delight, he longed to be up there with her, but was immensely worried he would fall off her back and plummet to his death.

"I will not let you fall, Arthur. That is a promise," Atheria said. "Find your bow and practise shooting."

Arthur went inside the hut, the once familiar scent overpowered by the sour stench of spilled ale, making itself comfortable among their meagre possessions. He scratched together a quick breakfast of stale bread and dried rabbit meat, chewing as quickly as he could.

The bow and quiver of arrows lay propped in the corner, next to his father's rusty sword in its leather sheath. He picked up the sheath, removing the sword and placed the axe in its place. As a child he had dreamed of having a warrior father, and in one sense it was true. His reality was, however, completely different. His father was all violence, no honour. Arthur had always believed his father had found the sword, or inherited it. Not once had he seriously entertained the fact his father could have used it in battle.

Rust coloured the blade, making the once-smooth surface rough beneath Arthur's fingers. Taking the handle in both hands, Arthur swung the blade, feeling its weight. Although it was heavy, Arthur could lift it easily, having become used to carrying heavy things. In the past, he had been forced to lug reluctant goats back home while they struggled mightily within his arms. With a final grunt of effort, Arthur brought the blade down into an empty ale barrel, relishing the sound it made as it wedged between the wooden planks.

Grabbing the sharpening stone he used on his arrowheads, he moved outside with the weapons, watching Atheria swoop and dive through the air while he sharpened the sword, scrubbing off the rust. Shiny iron appeared beneath the red dust, glinting in the sunlight.

Once the sword was cleaned and back in its sheath, Arthur sharpened the heads of his arrows. He had a full quiver, but wished for more. He practised shooting at various targets, getting all but one spot on. Nineteen out of twenty was a good success rate.

But they were stationary targets, and he was standing still.

"Try shooting while you are on my back," Atheria said, dropping to the ground in a flurry of wind. Arthur's stomach somersaulted like Atheria had just done as he thought of riding on her back. "Before you hop up, examine my body. Look for the weaknesses!"

Stepping closer to the dragon, Arthur ran his eyes over the spiky skin on her back. He reached out his hand, feeling the warmth before his hand even touched her. With a shaky finger Arthur prodded Atheria's skin between the conical spikes, harder than goat horns. He climbed onto her back and felt the tops of her wings. Every time Arthur pressed her hot skin, he felt no resistance. It felt as if he was pressing wood. Atheria's spikes were longer on top of her body than beneath her, and every point that Arthur tried was tough and unrelenting. He jumped down from her back.

"Well, I must say, you dragons are tough. Every inch of your skin is thick. Except for your eyes, ears and mouth, your body would be an impenetrable fortress to my arrows. I don't see how we will be able to defeat the others if they decide to fight against us." Arthur stared at the ground, his hand fiddling with his eggshell necklace, watching the long grass sway softly in the breeze.

"Perhaps our skin is weaker than you think. Of course, I will not allow you to try shooting me. You also have not tried my underside. Look here beneath my wing. And here on my belly, between the folds of skin." Atheria's claws scratched softly at her skin. "We are vulnerable. We can take arrows, don't despair. Our skin is tough, yes; however, it is less tough beneath us."

Arthur looked up, his eyebrows arched, feeling like herds of hopeful goats were dancing inside his chest. "Of course! I forgot to check beneath you! I feel ridiculous, but because you were crouching down, I just simply forgot to look."

Atheria stood on her hind legs, her wings flapping lightly to keep her balance. Her spikes were shorter than the tip of Arthur's little finger. When he pressed the skin, it was softer, more pliable. Hope began to grow inside his chest as he looked up at Atheria.

"We can do this! We can get them!"

"We must train you to ride my back. Quickly, Arthur. Climb up," Atheria urged.

Arthur grabbed the sheathed sword and buckled it around his waist. He hoped he wouldn't have need of it. Next he slung the bow and the quiver of arrows over his shoulder before climbing onto Atheria's back. There was a flat spot behind her neck, large enough for him to sit comfortably without spikes prodding his body. He sat with his legs hanging over her shoulders. Fortunately Atheria had large spikes protruding from her neck so Arthur could hold on and give his knees a break from digging in.

"Is that okay?" Arthur asked. "I'm not hurting you?"

"I have tough skin," Atheria replied. Arthur felt her body shake as Atheria flapped her wings, rising into the air. The wind rushed over Arthur's body as the ground plummeted away from them. White-knuckled, Arthur held on, his teeth clenched.

"Please relax, Arthur. Remember, I will not let you fall. That is a promise." Arthur loosened his grip and began to enjoy the ride as Atheria swooped through the air.

"Okay, Arthur, I am going to swoop down once more. I want you to hit that barrel there."

Nodding his consent, Arthur dug his knees in harder and grabbed his bow and an arrow. He felt the fletching as he put the nock on the string, drew it back and aimed. Atheria swooped, plummeting quickly. Shaking from the wind, Arthur loosed the arrow, before loading another and fired it soon after.

Both arrows missed their target. Arthur screamed in frustration.

"It is okay, Arthur. We shall practise until you hit the mark. Remember to focus on your target." Atheria rose up once more while Arthur prepared another arrow.

This time, as Atheria swooped, Arthur kept his eye on the target, steadying his arms against the airstream. Before his first arrow had hit the target, Arthur had loaded another and loosed it. Only the first arrow hit the barrel, but Arthur felt a sense of achievement. He had hit the mark. He had overcome his fear of flight and learned to trust Atheria's skill.

Glancing up at the horizon, he could see the smoke was getting thicker. The fire was obviously spreading as the dragons headed towards the castle. He remembered the traveller's last words as Atheria dropped to the ground: "Arrows will hit the mark".

Climbing off to retrieve his arrows, Arthur pondered the advice. Surely the king would have archers to protect his castle. Would they be able to slay the onslaught of dragons?

"We must hurry, Arthur. I sense my peers closing in on the kingdom." Arthur looked across at his father, still sprawled on the ground, his chest rising steadily with each breath. *Idiot*, thought Arthur.

After he had replaced the arrows in his quiver and had drunk some water, he climbed back onto Atheria and felt her rise into the air once more. She flew swiftly towards the smoky horizon, and Arthur watched the world pass beneath them, like a fast flowing river.

Ahead, the kingdom's outlying village came into view, its smouldering carcass lying dormant, surrounded by large, black rings. Arthur could see no signs of life except for the wisps of smoke still pouring from the burnt wood of what were once people's homes.

He hoped they had had time to flee.

"It seems my peers have wreaked havoc here. We must hurry on," Atheria said, increasing her speed. Arthur could smell the burnt tinge wafting through the air.

The woods surrounding the castle ahead were ablaze and, squinting, Arthur could see large shadows flying through the haze. Large silhouettes outlined by orange-tinted smoke.

On the ground below, Arthur saw a band of the king's knights in silver armour. They were mounted on warhorses, pointing up at the dragon above them.

"We should land and get news from those knights," Arthur said.

"I doubt they will take kindly to me, but if you think it is best then I will land," Atheria said, turning round and lowering them to the ground.

The knights drew their swords and moved forwards, ready to attack.

"Stop!" Arthur yelled. "I come in peace. We have come to help out the king and stop the dragons!"

"Then why are you on a dragon yourself?" one of the soldiers called, still moving towards them. A thick, black beard flowed out beneath the protective face plate of his helmet. Arthur sensed he was in charge.

"We bonded when Atheria, my dragon, hatched. We landed to learn of the dangers ahead before we fly on," Arthur said, desperate for the knight to believe him.

The knight laughed heartily. "The kingdom is about to fall. King George sent us away to find help, but the castle will be in ruins by the time we have returned. How can a kid and his pet help fight against four dragons, I'd like to know!" The knight turned to his soldiers. "Let's rid the world of a dragon, men!"

"Please, sir! We don't want to fight you. Atheria will burn you to a crisp if you get too close. We know how to kill the dragons. Do as your king says and find help. But find the help of healers; you will need them."

"Healers, you say? Healers to fix the damage you plan to make, kid?" Arthur found it hard to believe the soldier was still antagonistic. They had shown them no need for violence.

"How many dragons will we be up against? Has King George got archers? He will need them."

The soldiers still continued to move slowly forward, their swords held out in front of them. "We saw four of your fellow dragons. And yes, you will be up against archers. Not as many as I would have liked, but I am not in charge. Nobody listens to me; it is all swordplay for the King's guard."

Atheria blew a small ball of flame towards the approaching knights, and they baulked away, their arms raised protectively in front of their faces.

"Come no closer," Arthur said. "We mean you no harm, but will defend ourselves. Go! Go find healers, and we will fight the dragons." Atheria leapt into the air, turning back to the castle. He could hear the shouts of the soldiers behind him and hoped they would go find healers. Many would be needed if the kingdom survived the battle.

As they approached the outskirts of the castle, the burning forest beneath them, they saw chaos on the scorched clearing. Soldiers and civilians were running back and forth, avoiding the shooting flames, ducking for cover. Standing on the castle's fortification, bowmen shot arrows at the dragons flying around them. Arthur counted only three dragons, all bigger than Atheria. *Where is the other dragon?* Arthur wondered. The bowmen shouted from the rampart as a dragon dived, spurting flames.

Atheria flew high above the castle, still unnoticed by those fighting below. On the other side of the castle, the battle continued, and Arthur saw the fourth dragon. It lay on its side, a wing crumpled beneath its large body. A group of sword-wielding knights were stabbing it as they stood around, ensuring it remained on the ground. Arthur could just make out a number of arrows protruding from various sections of its body. One swordsman was hacking at the neck of the dragon, and stopped when Atheria's shadow swept over him. He looked up, calling out to the soldiers around him.

As they turned back to the action, Arthur saw a dragon flying towards its fallen comrade. When it saw the carcass, the dragon roared, spurting fire as it dived towards the huddle of soldiers, their swords held out before them. The flames engulfed them as the dragon picked some troops up in its sharp claws, before throwing them aside like a rag doll.

Arthur drew his bow, ready to fire when he saw the chance. If he could fell another dragon, they'd have two left. Perhaps they could try to create an alliance with them and call a truce.

The dragon below them demolished his hopes of a peaceful end as it looked up and saw Arthur on Atheria's back. A stream of flames hurtled towards them; Atheria dodged it with ease, turning to the side.

"It knows we are against them," Atheria said. "They will not back down, not until they have destroyed this kingdom and claimed it as their own."

The world was on fire around them, giving everything an orange tint in the dusk light. Atheria continued to swerve and duck, avoiding the dragon's flames as it gave chase, getting closer to them with each powerful flap of its wings.

Arthur peered behind them, bow and arrow in hand, ready to fire. He saw the approaching dragon and longed for a shot at it.

"You may only get one chance to shoot," Atheria said. "It is much faster than I am, and it will gain quickly when I turn mid-air. Are you ready?" Arthur braced himself and nodded.

"Now!" he called.

Without a moment's hesitation, Atheria dived, turned to face their descending opponent, her huge wings turning them effortlessly as they pounded back and forth. Arthur saw the belly of the dragon as it plunged towards them. He loosed two arrows in quick succession, aiming for the belly. He shot again, this time aiming for inside the dragon's open mouth.

Atheria dodged the plummeting dragon as it hurtled to the ground, its body limp. Ashes burst around the dragon as it hit the ground, its neck snapping to the side. Soldiers on the castle wall cheered, pumping their fists in the air. Arthur wondered if they had seen all the action, or just the destruction of their enemy. He hoped they knew he was on their side.

"Should we check to make sure it's dead?" Arthur asked as they hovered in the air.

"I sensed the life leave its body after your arrows. I believe the first two were mortal wounds, but your third seemed to finish it off. Well done, Arthur!" Atheria searched the skies for more of their foes within the smoke. "If it had been alive, the impact of hitting the ground would have finished it off. I heard the neck snap."

Arthur did the math in his head; he had seventeen arrows left with only two dragons. Hopefully it would be enough to complete the task.

A loud shriek pierced the sky, making the soldiers on the wall stop cheering and crouch for cover. Atheria's wing beats increased speed and they rose higher, searching for the dragon. Without warning, Atheria was flung to the side as the dragon swung its tail from behind. Its spiked end came within inches of hitting Arthur and knocking him off, dead. He reached for an arrow, his knees holding on strong while Atheria recovered from the attack. A wave of arrows shot up towards their opponent, each missing their mark, but they were enough to distract it, giving Atheria a chance to reclaim her position and fly upwards, away from immediate danger.

"That was close," Arthur said, his bow ready to fire.

"I cannot see through this haze. That hit almost knocked me down. I almost broke my promise to you, Arthur, and I apologise."

"You have nothing to apologise for. Let's go hunt that dragon." Although Arthur felt fear deep within him, he was ready to fight, confident in his ability with the bow. Confident with Atheria's skill.

"I am going to fly down to it. Get ready to shoot it in the eye, or wherever you can see for a target. You may not be able to get it in the belly. Also be ready to hold on, just in case it comes to a physical wrestling match."

"I'm ready," Arthur said. Atheria descended quickly, silently. The dragon was floating up to meet them and, upon seeing them coming towards it, braced in a defensive position. With a mighty roar, it flew backwards, and then pounced forwards, its claws meeting with Atheria's. She moved into a vertical position and Arthur put a hand out to grab a spike and stop himself from falling backwards.

The dragons clamoured for supremacy, their muscles tensing with the effort, about ten metres from the ground. Atheria was kicked multiple times in the belly, but remained firm, whipping her tail against her opponent. Arthur held on and waited for an opening, one moment where he could fire an arrow into a target. He knew he wouldn't have much time.

Atheria struggled free from the dragon's grasp and moved back, righting herself into a horizontal position, allowing more opportunities of attack and defence. Now was his chance.

Arthur fumbled with an arrow, his shaking hands struggling to get the notch on the string. Finally he had the bow loaded, searched for a target and shot, aiming for the dragon's belly once more. The dragon, seeing him aim, leaned forward protectively and the arrow ricocheted from the tough skin on the back of its neck. Loading another arrow, Arthur aimed for the eye, and missed once more. A shrieking roar sounded behind them, and a quick look showed the last dragon was zooming towards them.

The second dragon was smaller than the dragon in front of them, but had its mouth open, ready to blow fire towards them. Arthur pivoted his body, loading an arrow as he did, his body now facing Atheria's wing. Just as Arthur was about to fire, the first dragon moved forward to attack. Atheria moved to defend herself with her claws, which sent Arthur lurching sideways. He put an arm out to hold on until he found spikes large enough to stand on. Then, with his feet as firm in their position as he could manage, loaded an arrow and shot towards the descending dragon, aiming for its open mouth. He fired three arrows before Atheria was thrown back by a mighty blow, sending him hurtling towards the ground, back first.

At least one of his arrows had hit its mark; the dragon fell quickly to the ground, close by him. His last vision before he landed was of Atheria locked in close-quarter combat with the largest dragon, its jaw around her neck.

WHEN ARTHUR WOKE, THE air was still filled with an orange haze. The night had brought darkness to the land, the moon hidden behind a curtain of clouds. His head was filled with pain. Atheria was nowhere in sight. He lay on the ground, listening to the sounds of warfare around him. Shouts and thuds dominated the air. Cold drove its way through his threadbare clothes and he shivered, longing for the warmth of Atheria.

Where is she? he wondered. *How much time has passed?*

Arthur sat up slowly, feeling nauseous. With a churn of his stomach, he leaned over and vomited next to his bow. *At least it's not broken.* His quiver was on the other side, the arrows scattered around him. One had broken in the fall. The sword was still in its sheath around his waist.

After collecting his arrows—fourteen left now—Arthur stood up slowly, his legs wobbly beneath him. He drank the last of his water from his pouch, washing away the taste of vomit, and surveyed the burnt land around him. He could see the dragons scattered close by, slain by arrows. The traveller had been right about that. *But where is Atheria?*

He moved over to the last dragon he had hit, green blood oozing from its cold mouth. Its eyes were open, staring disconcertingly at him. They saw nothing, but looked ever on at the destruction it had caused.

Overcome with a sudden rage, Arthur drew his sword and drove it deep into the dragon's eye, yellow slime gushing out. After withdrawing his sword, Arthur wiped it on the dragon's wing, yellow streaks smeared among the orange glow reflected on the blade. With the sword back in its sheath and his anger subsided, Arthur stumbled toward the castle wall, looking for Atheria, listening for her voice.

He walked along the wall, glad for what little shelter it provided him. He heard the distant roar of a dragon and hurried forward, hoping Atheria was safe. Three dragons lay dead behind him, and it seemed the other was still alive. It was going to be a long night.

Even though the sun had gone down, the orange haze lit up the ground like a foggy day.

"Arthur." His name was barely audible, whispered softly as if breathed. *She is alive!* "Arthur."

"Atheria?" Arthur called, stroking his medallion. "Where are you?"

"Follow your instinct. I am close by." Arthur moved quickly, some unknown intuition kicking in to guide him. A large mound appeared ahead of him and Arthur, sensing his friend, rushed forward.

Atheria lay unmoving but for the slight rise and fall of her laboured breathing. Green blood trickled from wounds in her neck.

"Atheria! What happened? Are you okay?" Arthur said, his heart beating fast inside his chest.

"I... fought but... was wounded... Toxic bite... You must... finish the... fight... without me..." Arthur felt tears forming in his eyes, unsure what to do. He needed to get inside the castle walls; he needed a healer.

"I'm not going to let you die! I'm going to find a healer to help." Arthur rushed towards the gate, waving his arms to gain the attention of the gatekeeper.

"Who are you?" a booming voice demanded. "Where is your armour?"

"Please, I need help! I need a healer," Arthur pleaded.

"All the healers are busy. Can't you see the destruction around you? Unless you're going to help with that bow, I demand you leave at once!"

"I *can* help! I slew two of the dragons. I have arrows left for the last, but we are doomed if my own dragon steed dies." Arthur paused, letting the knowledge sink in. "You need my dragon to fight. Please!"

There was no answer. Arthur banged his fists against the gate in frustration. *Why won't they listen?* Overwhelmed with desperation, Arthur looked for a way in. Gigantic stone walls ran as far as he could see in both directions, and the wooden gate in front of him looked as thick as giant oak trunks.

The doors began to rattle and clank and the doors started to budge slowly, whirring loudly as they swung outwards. Arthur stepped back and waited.

A man in dark robes stepped through the crack, just as the doors began to close again, a loud bang echoing through the air as they were locked once more.

"I was told you need a healer, boy. You look well enough."

"No, sir. My dragon... Atheria... She's been injured. You need to help her. I need to return to the fight and she's bleeding and weak."

"A dragon on your side, you say? And what side are you on?" The healer's brows were furrowed beneath his hood. He carried a leather satchel over his shoulder, holding on tight as if it was full of gold and treasures.

"I fight for the king, sir. We slayed two dragons before... Before she was injured. Please hurry! This way!" The healer followed Arthur to where Atheria lay injured on the battlefield. Rain began to fall while they walked, drenching them completely.

"I have with me sap from a Hurbrus tree. It works on human skin, and mends large wounds quickly, restoring the injured person. Expensive stuff. I have some other basic herbs and potions I use with minor cuts, scratches and snake bites. But I cannot guarantee they will work on a dragon. It is most peculiar for me, most peculiar!"

"We must try everything we can. There she is," Arthur said as they approached Atheria. He blinked through the rain dripping into his eyes and could see steam rising from Atheria's motionless body. Arthur watched as the healer tended to her wounds, glancing occasionally into the distance where the forest fires were easing off. The final dragon was nowhere in sight, and Arthur hoped it had moved on to another kingdom, never to return.

The healer muttered as he worked, giving him a mystical appearance, the fog rising in tendrils around him. Ancient words floated through the air, making Arthur overwhelmed with curiosity.

Finally the healer turned to Arthur, his face grim. "I have done all that I can for her. The wound is glued closed and I have fused both ancient and modern techniques to ward off poisons and infections. She must rest now."

"But there must be something else I can do!" Arthur exclaimed, watching Atheria's chest rise ever so slightly with her struggled breaths.

"Here, take these. It's all the healing herbs I have left. If she wakes, put some of these leaves into her mouth. They may help to energise her. Otherwise, there is nothing else to do. Now I must be going. Good luck!" The healer passed Arthur the herbs from his satchel and hurried back to the castle gates. Arthur watched him leave; the healer did not look back.

Arthur knelt beside Atheria and stroked her head, feeling the rough skin beneath his fingers. Water trickled into her mouth and nose as she breathed. The steam increased around her body as the rain continued to fall. He felt tears mix with the rain on his cheeks as he leaned his head against his dragon's.

"Please don't die," he sobbed. "I need you."

Suddenly, a great roar reverberated through the air and Arthur looked up, terrified. The other dragon was coming back! Retrieving an arrow from its quiver, he loaded his bow, ready to defend Atheria. He could see the last dragon on the horizon, blowing fire at groups of soldiers as it flew low to the ground. If it continued on its path, the dragon would fly right over him and he would have the perfect shot.

The dragon veered away. Arthur relaxed the bow, swearing under his breath. A small part of him wanted to rush off to slay the dragon, however, he didn't want to leave Atheria's side.

"Damn everyone else," he said. "I'm not going to leave you, Atheria."

Her eyes blinked open as he spoke, startling him. Atheria breathed loudly, blowing steam heavily from her nostrils.

"I need water... and food," Atheria said as Arthur looked deep within her eyes.

"You're awake!" Arthur exclaimed, a smile forming on his lips. He took the herbs the healer had given him and put them to her mouth. "The healer who tended to your wounds said to give you this."

Atheria's rough lips nibbled at his hand, swallowing the last of the herbs. They were motionless as the herbs made their way to Atheria's stomach.

Slowly, Atheria pushed herself onto her claws, standing up woozily. "The final dragon is near. We must be careful," Arthur said.

"It has... moved into... the distance," Atheria said. "I will... be back." Grunting in pain, Atheria jumped into the air and flew off into the orange haze, growing darker as the rain fell.

Arthur had never felt so alone. He had spent his entire existence surrounded by nobody except his bleating goats. In fact, he had enjoyed the serenity. But in the short time he had known Atheria, he had grown to rely on her presence, on her friendship. To have her almost die, and then fly off soon after she had recovered, wreaked havoc on his feelings.

A figure was approaching from across the field on horseback, galloping through the downpour. Arthur watched, intrigued. Were they coming towards him? Or away from something?

Loud roaring sounded on Arthur's right side, making him turn in terror. The final dragon was once more attempting to destroy everything in its path as it flew towards Arthur, this time making no apparent effort to turn. A stream of fire blew forth from its massive jaws. Preparing his bow, Arthur watched, looking for a target. Any exposed area would be enough as the dragon flew overhead.

And if Arthur died in the process... Well, so be it. He would die with honour defending his kingdom. Even if his kingdom had done nothing to help him. He could hear the sound of the horse splashing through the puddles behind him. Chancing a glance behind him, Arthur saw the man was in full armour, a sword held in his right hand. The man roared as he charged, fighting to be heard over the torrential rain and the thunderous rumble of the dragon.

"Duck, Arthur," the soldier yelled as he drew up alongside him. The voice was strangely familiar and Arthur thought hard to place it, while watching the dragon's progress towards them. The horse galloped to the left, turning easily. Arthur dropped to the ground, obeying the order, his bow and arrow lying awkwardly in the mud in front of him.

Finally, the cogs of his mind locked into place, and he recognised the voice. Overwhelmed by surprise, he realised it was his father. *What's he doing here?* Arthur wondered.

His father's horse swerved through the mud, the dragon upon its tail, looming over them as the stallion straightened its path. Then, without warning, Arthur's father jumped up on the horse's back, turned on his foot and swung the sword, chopping off one of the dragon's front claws.

Dark green blood spurted from the wound as Arthur watched, transfixed in awe of his father's swordsmanship.

The dragon bellowed, stopping quickly, its mighty wings beating fast. Then, it blew fire towards its opponent, igniting Richard and his horse. The flames licked hungrily across their skin and, as Arthur's father fell heavily off the horse, he rolled in the puddles beneath him, quelling the fire.

Sensing its opponent's demise, the dragon flew off, booming thunderously as it went. Arthur ran to his father, overcome with guilt. The horse lay beside his father, a smouldering pile of flesh. There was still some small life left in Arthur's father, but not much. His chest was rising in small gasps, before collapsing heavily. Arthur could hear the breaths, like ragged whispers and, when Arthur moved closer, he could make out some quiet words escaping from between the lips, which were burnt back to the crimson muscle and white bones.

"Sorry." The word came so softly that Arthur almost missed it. When he did hear it, he thought he had imagined it. But the word was definitely there.

His father had saved him, and apologised. But for what? The years of mistreatment? For his alcoholism? For dying?

A tempestuous roar sounded on the horizon, ending Arthur's brief moment of grief. He prepared his bow, ready to shoot if the dragon was returning. As he watched, he sensed, rather than saw, Atheria's majestic form returning. *She's back!* Arthur thought, relaxing his bow.

Arthur's heart filled with joy. He watched as she soared over his head, turned around and glided to the ground.

"I am not fully recovered; that will take some time. But I am healed enough to fight once more. I sense the other dragon has been wounded. What transpired here?"

Arthur recounted what had happened, pointing to his father's burnt body as he described his death.

"He was a very brave man. To rush into battle against a fearsome beast to defend the life of another is no small feat. We must honour his sacrifice when this war is over." Atheria's voice was solemn as she spoke the small eulogy.

"We must avenge his death by destroying the dragon. Arthur, climb upon my back and we will depart to complete our attack. Before we leave, I want you to know it has been an honour to spend my only living day fighting with you."

"Thanks, Atheria. You have given me a reason to live again and, although my dad is dead, I feel the closest to him I have ever felt. He... He saved my life." Arthur wiped away a tear that began to crawl down his cheek. He climbed upon her back, feeling as if it was the last time he would do so. He hoped it wasn't a premonition of their deaths.

Once Arthur was safely in place on her back, Atheria spread her large wings, lifting them skywards. Below them, Arthur could see small fires struggling to survive against the raindrops. Although the rain had eased, it was still falling steadily, making Arthur's hair stick to his head. He blinked the rain from his eyes, squinting through the downpour for their opponent. His bow was armed and ready to shoot when he saw a target.

As they flew away, Arthur sensed a weakness in Atheria's flying ability, slowing her down. It was faint, but definitely there. If she was in pain, she hid it well. Arthur kept his eyes focussed for the other dragon, hopeful of one distinct advantage: the other dragon had lost its claw and would have also lost a lot of blood. Atheria, having been patched up, should have the advantage in a fair fight. But it could come at a huge cost to them both.

Atheria circled the battlefield, much darker due to the rain, making it hard to see too far into the distance. The smell of smoke mingled with the petrichor and the metallic scent of blood. Arthur's heart thudded heavily in his chest. He could see the looming dark shape of the castle below them, but no evidence of the dragon. Had it fled to lick its wounds? Or was it hiding among the shadows, ready to pounce as they flew past?

"I sense it nearby; I can hear it breathing," Atheria said. Atheria veered to the right, evading a spurt of flames from the left. She grunted in pain as her body moved to avoid the danger. Arthur held on, ready to shoot, but the flames had gone, leaving only darkness in his vision. The shadows would make it hard to see his target; he would have to rely on Atheria's superior senses to see their opposition.

If only the rain would go away, he would have some light to guide him. Looking up at the clouds, Arthur wished they would part, allowing the moon's light to wash over the ground below. He could feel his arrows itching to be released, to find their target. The wind rushed past him, freezing his soaked body. If it wasn't for Atheria's warmth, he would be frozen solid.

A rumble sounded behind them, the sound of large wings beating. Arthur looked back, seeing only black. Sensing danger, Atheria flew up, evading the stream of fire that followed them. They seemed to fly up for an extremely long time, the dragon close behind them. Arthur had begun to wonder how high they were when the rain was replaced with a translucent mist, and they broke through the clouds, the moon now clearly visible as Atheria straightened her path horizontally.

Breathing a sigh of relief, Arthur looked back. The dragon had followed them up, the clouds a sea of bubbles beneath them. Moonlight shone on the creature's back, revealing razor sharp spikes and rough skin.

Arthur loosed his bow, aiming for the dragon's eye, but missed, the arrow glancing off its ear. It slowly gained on them, Atheria flying at full speed, knowing they would lose ground if she tried to outmanoeuvre their foe. Arthur could feel her muscles struggling to propel them forward, knowing she grew weaker with each beat of her wings. Now that he could see in the silver light, Arthur observed the dragon's missing front claw, the wound having scabbed over, blood slowly dripping through the clouds.

A burst of fire spewed towards them, and Atheria swerved to the left and up, twisting quickly to loop behind their adversary. When Arthur saw the soft spot of its lower belly from their position just below, he took a shot, hitting the leg. The arrow ricocheted into the night sky. The dragon, distracted by its stream of fire, searched the sky uncertainly, tracking its prey.

Fuelled by his frustration, Arthur focussed on the dragon, his eyes flicking back and forth, searching for a target. Any target, as long as the arrow would stick. Atheria continued swerving, trying to avoid detection. The dragon's roar sounded like thunder in the air, making Arthur wonder what the people below must be imagining.

The dragon saw them, pirouetting mid-air.

"Hold on, Arthur!" Atheria said as they came up to the halted dragon. Arthur grabbed her spikes, bow in hand, as Atheria performed a perfect barrel roll, her belly copping the full brunt of a burst of fire, the flames licking round her, searching eagerly for fuel.

Atheria gasped as she winced in pain, diving below the clouds, ready to reappear above in an unexpected location.

"I have been scratched, Arthur. It does not seem very deep."

"Try to get me to a weak spot, and I'll have it," Arthur replied, reloading another arrow.

With a burst of energy, Atheria rocketed skywards, back through the clouds, continuing to climb. The dragon was paused in wait, forced to watch as they ascended, before giving chase. Finally, when Atheria thought she had gone high enough, she stopped, waiting for their opponent, the morning sun beginning to brighten the horizon in front of them. Arthur peered around her, hoping to find a target. Rocketing towards them, the dragon kept its soft spots well-guarded. Its mouth was open, ready to spurt fire.

Arthur took aim and fired, but the dragon, predicting the move, closed its mouth. The arrow scraped its chin, coming to rest in the crease beneath its wing. Every time the dragon beat its wing, the arrow pushed deeper into its thick hide.

Wounded, the dragon beat its wings with less force, trying to avoid pushing the arrow in any deeper. It paused, its remaining front claw trying to grab hold of the shaft, distracted from its attack.

Arthur saw an opportunity, one that filled him with an overwhelming sense of fear. If he jumped now, he would have a perfect opportunity to fill the dragon's belly with arrows as he plummeted. He knew when they began the fight that he could die, but as his heart thumped in his chest, he didn't know if he could build the courage to jump. Atheria would try to catch him, but would she be able to? She had been injured and was suffering from exhaustion.

He had to try.

"Catch me, Atheria! I trust you," Arthur said as he bent his knees, bow in hand.

Arthur jumped. The wind stormed his body as he fell, but his eyes remained focussed on the still-distracted dragon's belly. Although it required more strength, Arthur was able to shoot his arrows as he fell, beginning from a high angle, counting down until he was no longer in range.

"Eleven," he began, breathless with the terror of the fall.

"Ten. Nine. Eight. Seven. Six." With each shot, he watched the dragon's belly become a pincushion. Watched as the dragon twitched with each shot into its soft skin.

"Five."

Just as he was about to fall through the clouds, he saw both dragons shooting towards him. Their enemy fell with its back to the ground; Atheria, face first, diving to catch her fallen rider.

The darkness enveloped Arthur as he fell, the wind thundering loudly in his ears. All senses had been ripped from him. Everything but the taste of fear as he rushed closer to the ground.

I must be almost to the ground, Arthur thought gloomily, resigned to his early death. Then, he came to a shuddering halt, a flurry of wings and leathery skin ending his descent. Somehow he avoided Atheria's larger spikes, but felt small ones prick his skin through his clothes. He dropped his bow as he scrambled to hold on to whatever he could grab, welcoming the warmth of Atheria's body beneath him. Something solid to replace the empty void.

"I think we should get some rest. Once we have ensured the dragon is dead, of course," Atheria said, her voice music to Arthur's ears. When her claws had found solid ground, Arthur breathed a sigh of relief and climbed down, his legs shaking. He held out his hand to steady himself. The rain had finally eased, the clouds thin, allowing the morning sun to paint the burnt ground in a dark grey. His body was filled with pain from the fall.

The dragon had fallen not far from where they stood, a black silhouette in the pale light. Arthur saw his bow on the ground beside him and picked it up, a familiar friend in his shaking hands. Then, after a few deep breaths to gather his strength, Arthur hobbled over to the dragon. He could feel the medallion, warm against his chest. Once he was close enough, he saw the eyes open, glazed and lifeless. Steam rose from the carcass, its jaw opened wide, revealing a mouth of sharp teeth.

Arthur grabbed an arrow and loaded it, staring into the dragon's eyes.

"This is for Emilica," he said, shooting the arrow into its eye. "This is for the soldiers you have killed." An arrow now protruded from the other eye.

"This is for wounding Atheria." Arthur shot another arrow into the first eye. "This one's for me." The dragon now had two arrows in each eye.

"And this one is for my father, may he rest in peace." Arthur squatted down and aimed the shot deep down its gullet. All Arthur had left of his father were his sword and a pile of bad memories.

Satisfied, he slung his bow over his shoulder and returned to Atheria, who waited patiently.

"Let's get some sleep," Arthur said as he climbed onto Atheria's back.

As they flew towards Arthur's home, the morning sunlight illuminated the world around them, making it seem like it was ablaze to their bleary eyes. A new day was dawning, and Arthur was truly happy for the first time in his life.

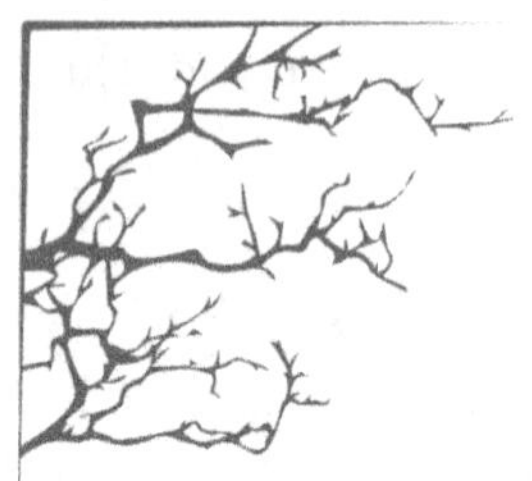

Lizzie

The wind blew through the caravan awning, threatening to rip it from its moorings. Loukas cringed with each gust, staring at the site around him. He never trusted his own skills of setting up the caravan for their yearly holiday by the beach, and yet each time they packed up, he was glad it had held.

"Stop stressing, Loukas," Melina said from across the plastic table. "It'll hold. There's nothing you can do." She took a sip of wine from her plastic cup. Everything was plastic, durable. They wanted their stuff to be safe while they towed their caravan around. Not to mention keeping their daughter Isabel protected from breakable crockery.

"I know, Mel, but the wind is super strong today." Loukas looked over at Isabel, who was sitting on the mat playing with a toy truck. He smiled, glad she wasn't into girly toys.

"You say that every year. Remember the storm left over from the cyclone last year? All that happened was the marquee flap pulled away from your clamp. It'll hold." Melina watched the orange netting dance in the wind. When she saw the little girl across the road run away from her parents, Melina was glad to have erected the barricade to hold their daughter. *Like a free-range chicken,* she thought.

Loukas ate the last of his sausage, looking down at the hopeful lizard on the ground. It peered up at him, its head tilted to gain a better view. He kicked out to scare it, but the reptile didn't even flinch. Instead, it took a few steps closer to the table, making Melina pull her feet up in fright.

"Good to see these lizard bastards haven't changed," Loukas muttered. Every year, the lizards had crowded around them, hoping for food. This year, Loukas and Melina were worried how they would go with Isabel toddling around.

"They're Australian water dragons. Harmless carnivores, apparently. Rodents, small birds, that sort of thing." Loukas held his phone out for Melina to see the images on Google.

"They still creep the hell outta me," Melina said. Isabel squealed and ran to Loukas, her arms outstretched. He placed his phone on the table, picked her up, and sat her on his lap.

"Lizzie!" she said, pointing down at the spiky reptile. She began to sob, her chest heaving. Tears flowed down her cheeks as a loud shriek escaped her throat.

"It's okay, Isabel. The lizard won't get you. You're safe, and you're loved," Loukas soothed, placing his face in her blonde hair, breathing in the scent of her curly locks. "You say, 'Go away, lizard!' and we can stomp our feet to get rid of it." Loukas began stamping his feet, Isabel kicking out on his lap.

"Go 'way, Lizzie!" Isabel squealed. The water dragon ran towards the permanent caravan site next to them and crawled between the wooden lattice.

"We need to do something about her fear," Loukas said, looking at Melina over his beer can. "We can't have her screaming at it every time it comes close to us."

"I can't help when they crawl over my feet," Melina said, defensive. Her glare could have sliced the leftover sausage cooling on the portable camping grill.

"I don't mean you, though it can't help. What if we let her feed it?" Loukas said, trying to ease the tension. The last thing he wanted was a fight on their holiday.

"That might help her get used to the creatures, but won't it just encourage them to keep coming back?" Melina took a sip of wine, staring at the lizard, which had just started to creep towards them again, as if the smell of sausages wafted on the strong winds, enticing it out. Isabel's sobs had quietened to hiccups, drowned out by the creaking annex around them.

"Well, keeping them hungry hasn't helped previously. They must be fed by other people who stay in this spot during the year," Loukas said. He passed a small piece of sausage to Isabel, encouraging her to feed the lizard. She held her arm behind her, before throwing it forwards. The meat fell about thirty centimetres away from Loukas' foot.

Tilting its head, the lizard eyed the meat, deciding whether it was worth the risk. Finally, it scurried forward and grabbed the meat, chewing it awkwardly in its mouth. Isabel squealed at its proximity to Loukas' leg, tears still threatening to fall down her face.

"It's okay, sweetie. Look, he's thanking you for the food," he said calmly in her ear. "Here, look! He won't hurt you." Loukas held out another piece of sausage for the lizard, which had just finished the first bit.

Loukas heard rustling in the grass and looked toward the lattice, keeping the meat in his hand. Two more lizards came out, their black eyes searching for food as they crept toward their friend.

"I told you the food would just encourage them," Melina said, taking another sip of wine. "I'm going inside where they can't come near me." Melina stood up, picking up her glass and dirty plate.

Loukas watched her go through the shaking annex into the caravan, before throwing the meat towards the two new lizards. They began fighting for the morsel, their jaws snapping at each other. Loukas noticed the winner had peeling skin along its body, and was slightly larger than the other. The smaller lizard began creeping towards where Loukas sat. Isabel began to squirm as she pivoted off her father's leg.

"I go with Mum," she said as she waddled quickly into the caravan. Loukas shook his head; he just wanted her to be more confident with new things. He didn't want to raise a child who had no resilience. He broke apart the rest of the sausage and, placing it onto his palm, held it down to the lizards, which were now only a hand span away from his foot.

As if sensing danger, they tilted their heads and rushed towards the meat, taking the chunks in open jaws. Loukas felt a tinge of pain and, when he looked down, he saw blood seeping from a small cut.

"Bastard!" he said, bringing his hand up to look closely at his wound. A lizard had nipped his hand; the three reptiles munching on their meat, still watching him greedily as they chewed. Loukas drank the last of his beer, grabbed his plate and moved inside to find the first aid kit.

"Honey, where is the first aid kit?" Loukas asked as he stepped into the caravan, bending forward to avoid hitting his head on the low doorway. Melina was lying on the bed, Isabel jumping excitedly beside her.

"Why? What happened?" Melina asked, sitting up on the bed in alarm. Loukas held out his hand, showing her the blood, a goofy expression on his face. "Oh my God, you're bleeding!"

Melina began to wriggle off the bed. Isabel continued jumping. Loukas grabbed some tissues to stem the flow of blood.

"The uh... The lizard kinda bit me when I fed it," Loukas mumbled as Melina grabbed the first aid kit.

"Isabel, stop jumping, please!" Melina said through gritted teeth as she rummaged in the khaki bag. Finally, Melina pulled out the bottle of antiseptic cream and a sticking plaster to cover the wound. She moved over to Loukas, who was sitting at the small table, holding the tissue on his hand.

"Now, I don't want to hear you complain about the pain. This will sting," Melina said, laying out the items. After pouring herself another glass of wine, Melina drank deeply. "I bloody knew those lizards would be dangerous. You're lucky it wasn't Izzy." Wine gone, she placed the cup on the table and picked up the antiseptic cream. She squeezed a generous amount on her husband's wound, relishing the gasps and wincing movements he made.

As Melina placed the plaster on the wound, they heard a loud commotion outside, as if dozens of people were holding a meeting on the road.

"What's happening?" Loukas said, standing up while Melina washed her hands. Peering out the mesh window, Loukas saw a group of people bent down, playing with the orange netting.

He turned to his wife and whispered, "They're playing with our barricade." Melina raised one of her eyebrows, a trick he had been unable to copy. Loukas looked back through the window, this time more carefully. Caught in one of the holes of the plastic netting was a water dragon, double the size of the others. It writhed and squirmed, unable to free its trapped body.

Loukas narrated the events for Melina. "I should probably go out and free it, I guess," Loukas muttered, glancing sourly at his wounded palm. "Where are the scissors?"

Melina pointed to a shelf above the sink. "Just there, where you left them." Isabel giggled as Melina grabbed her around the waist and jumped into bed, pulling her daughter onto her chest. Loukas smiled as he grabbed the scissors and stepped out through the annex into the bright sun. The wind whipped through his hair.

Some of the people had left; only a few kids on bikes remained. They stared at the lizard as if it was a zoo exhibit. Loukas moved over to the netting and squatted down. He felt the weight of many eyes focussed on his head as he reached out to grab the barricade. Whispered comments carried on the wind, blending in to make white noise in his ears. Behind them the sun was setting, surrounded by clouds that appeared to be preventing its descent, as if they were scared of the dark. The water dragon thrashed in its wild attempt to escape; its jaws opened and shut viciously.

Loukas held the scissors out, hoping to avoid cutting the reptile. He could imagine how badly that would go down with the children who watched his every move. No doubt one of them was recording on their phone, though he was too focussed on cutting the creature free to look up. He pulled his hand back as the lizard tried to bite the scissors.

With his left hand, Loukas held the netting up, hoping the lizard would drop out and be free. Its front legs were scrabbling in the grass trying to pull itself through, its elbows pulled back against the plastic. Concentrating on his aim, Loukas snipped the plastic around the lizard and it fell backwards, free from its trap. The kids on the bike, realising the excitement was over, took one last look and began to move away.

Thankful for the lack of observers, Loukas watched the lizard as it shook its body and stared back at him. It raised one foot and scratched its head, before waving the claws quickly at Loukas, who was sure it wasn't thanking him enthusiastically. The snapping jaws were a bit of a giveaway there. Loukas stood up and moved back inside, out of the fierce wind, which had begun to grow cold.

"Well, it's free. Bloody thing tried to eat the scissors!" Loukas said as he entered the caravan. Melina and Isabel were asleep on the bed, wrapped in a loose embrace. Smiling, he stood watching them sleep, before grabbing a beer and sitting at the table, scrolling through his phone and nibbling on macadamia nuts.

As darkness surrounded him and his empty beer cans multiplied, Loukas felt like he could join his family in sleep. After visiting the toilet block, Loukas moved Isabel to her own bed on the couch, before climbing in next to his wife.

The wind flowed through the caravan, keeping the air fresh and cool, though it was less intense than it was outside. With the annex zipped shut, they left the caravan door open, joining in with the rest of the caravan community. Everybody trusted everyone else; important if you chose to use a tent. Not to mention how loud the zip was when it was opened; even slowly, it screamed into the night. Isabel's nightlight provided enough to see into both the caravan and the annex.

"Thank you," Melina slurred. Loukas smiled at his wife passed out next to him. His own eyes felt heavy and, as his head hit the pillow, he felt sleep come quickly.

A STRANGE SCRATCHING sound pulled Loukas from a deep sleep. He looked around the dimly lit caravan, his breathing stopped to hear more clearly. Sitting up, Loukas saw nothing in the annex or the caravan. Outside, stillness echoed through the wind, buffeting against their site.

"What's the matter?" Melina asked groggily.

"I thought I heard a scratching noise," he said, still peering around the dimly lit space. "Must have just been the wind."

He laid his head on the pillow and closed his eyes. As he began to drift back to sleep, he heard more scratching, this time louder and more consistent, getting closer. The sheets began to fall down the end of the bed. When Loukas tried to pull them back up, they felt weighted, heavy.

Loukas bolted upright and tugged harder, the scratching noise increasing. Finally he pulled the sheets back onto the bed, amazed at what was attached.

Staring at him from the end of the bed was the large lizard he had freed from the netting outside. Loukas flicked on the bedside lamp, unable to believe his eyes. When he saw the floor of the caravan, Loukas regretted his decision of more light.

On the floor were what looked like hundreds of water dragons, all scrabbling for a better position. Some of them had begun climbing up onto the couch where Isabel lay sleeping, others were crawling towards the bed, where they climbed to join the large lizard leader among the tangles of bedsheets.

The large lizard bit Loukas' big toe, making him scream in pain.

"What's happening?" Melina asked, more alert this time. She put her hand on her husband's arm. "What's wrong?"

Loukas continued screaming, kicking out frantically at the growing number of lizards. The bed was wet and, when Melina looked down, she gasped. Loukas' toe was missing, bitten off. Blood spurted from the wound, soaking into the bed. The large reptile was gnawing on the toe, fending off other lizards trying to steal its prize.

Melina squealed as a smaller lizard tried unsuccessfully to bite off her toe. She kicked quickly, as if running on the spot for a work-out. Some of the lizards were knocked off, only to be replaced by even more of the creatures.

Isabel moaned from her bed, where more lizards had climbed, crawling onto her legs and torso. Melina began to sit up, only to be thrown down by the weight of many water dragons crawling onto her, their claws digging deep into her skin, leaving bloody pockmarks. More reptiles came through the door like a tidal wave, crawling on top of other lizards to get to the fresh meat, attracted by the metallic scent of blood.

Melina could feel claws and teeth maul her skin, biting the flesh and sucking the blood. Her own shrieks drowned out the squeals of terror from her husband and daughter.

Outside, the wind raced through the air, carrying away the unheard screams from inside the caravan until they dissipated into the atmosphere.

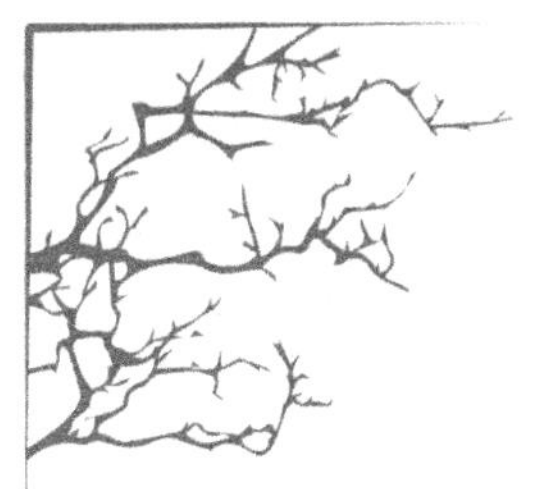

Insomnia

Macy's head felt heavy as her eyes fluttered open, squinting against the morning sunlight breaking into the room. No matter which pills Macy took—both prescribed and self-medicated—sleep still evaded her. Every morning was the same: zombified brain and itchy eyes, and a massive lack of enthusiasm for the day ahead.

Staring at the ceiling, Macy listened to the sleepy sounds of the town outside. Birds began their musical chorus; wind blew the trees in a rhythmic, swaying dance. Macy found it strange that she heard no cars driving by. Usually the morning brought a stream of cars and trucks rumbling past on the nearby highway, on their way to work. A man-made discord, now routine and out of place.

A glance at her phone showed Macy it was still not time for her to wake up. Her alarm still had twenty minutes to go. She scrolled through her social media feed, annoyed at the old news greeting her day, yet unable to draw her attention away to the real world.

When her alarm finally chirped, the cheery song unaware of Macy's dark mood, she switched it off and began to struggle out of bed. She sat on the side, her head resting in her hands, rubbing her bleary eyes. With a grunt of effort, she stood up and padded around the house, preparing for work. Her mornings were habitually plagued with thoughts of taking a sickie, but she wanted to save up her leave for a rainy day. *Not that we ever get any rain*, she thought, annoyed by the dryness around her. Droughts turned gardening into incredibly arduous work.

Macy peered out the front window, observing the houses and gardens, but no sign of human movement. *Is it somehow the weekend?* Macy thought. Her phone said it was Wednesday, hump day. The small, rural town should be a bustling hive of activity, but it was as quiet as it was at night, when nearly everyone stayed at home. Even the sky was nearly empty; a small splotch of cloud covering luminous blue as if someone had tried to remove graffiti, leaving only a stain of white.

Once Macy was ready for work, she headed out the door, handbag slung over her shoulder. The absence of machine noise outside spooked her. She had thought that at least one other person would be awake and moving by eight o'clock. Students and teachers had school to go to; retail assistants had shops to prepare; drivers had trucks full of products to distribute.

But not today.

Today, the streets were deserted. Cars had been left in random positions on the road, and Macy drove slowly around them, peering in as she crawled past. She was not going to get out of her car to check more carefully. Macy wouldn't have been surprised to see tumbleweeds rolling past like in the old cartoons she watched as a child. Even her favourite coffee shop, which usually opened at sparrow's fart, was closed. She sat in her idling car, peering in through the storefront windows. Had the town caught some kind of sleeping disease which Macy, an insomniac, had been immune to?

Something is wrong, Macy thought, peering around, looking for any sign of life. She saw a flash of movement in her car's mirror, a shadow within the darkness of the alleyway. When she had turned around in her seat to look more carefully, there was nothing. The darkness remained stagnant, a shadow of the street outside. A shiver vibrated down Macy's spine; goose bumps formed on her skin. Macy shook her head, blinked, tried to clear the eerie feeling from her mind.

With the sudden realisation that the town's service stations were always open, she began to drive eagerly towards her favourite one, which was also the closest to her. She loved chatting to Manager Marge, an old school friend. Six years ago, it had been Maggie; but she had grown out of that nickname, and into the managing role at the servo.

Macy parked near the door, leaving her car running. If anything was out of the ordinary inside, then she would be able to—hopefully—make a speedy getaway. There were more cars sitting dormant in the carparks around her, and on the highway. The town's one set of traffic lights still changed, directing the empty streets, ignorant of the absence of normality around them.

Something strange had happened, as if she had not woken from some horrible nightmare. Yet it all seemed too real. She felt every wisp of wind, smelled the slightly alluring scent of petrol. She even pinched herself like they did in the children's horror books she had read when she was younger.

Still the scene did not change.

Inside the service station, everything was quiet. The shelves were still stocked with overpriced items. The fridges were still illuminating the cool drinks inside. The cameras still stalked the aisles. All normal, as it should be.

Except for the absence of people.

Macy walked to the counter and peered behind. Maggie was lying prostrate on the floor, one arm bent in a strange angle beneath her.

"Maggie! Wake up! Are you okay?" Macy called out. She was unable to get in to see her. The counter was protected by wires; the door was locked. Protected from criminals, and CPR.

"Marge! Maggie! What happened?" Still, Maggie remained lying motionless on the tiles. Macy pulled her phone from her jeans pocket, peering through the windows into the street as she dialled the emergency services.

"Come on! Pick up, pick up. Pick up!" she said into the phone. The phone continued to ring.

Macy looked back at Maggie, willing her to wake up. Willing everything to be back to normal. She rubbed her eyes—harder than usual—listening to the repetitive dial tones in her ear, stars appearing behind her eyelids. She was so tired, her mind fuzzy. When she opened her eyes again, she thought she saw a flash of shadow pass the bowsers in her peripheral vision. It looked like some kind of monstrous figure, tall and alien.

I'm seeing things. I've finally gone crazy from lack of sleep, she thought. A closer look revealed nothing out of the ordinary.

A loud recurring beep sounded in her ear. The phone call had rung out. "What the Hell?" she exclaimed. *The emergency number is always answered, isn't it?*

Promising to pay for it later, Macy grabbed an iced coffee bottle from the fridge, drinking half in one gulp. As the milk sloshed around in her stomach, she tried ringing Triple Zero again. She felt sick, unsure whether it was the sweet milk or her current situation.

"Maggie, wake up!" she called again. Her friend remained unresponsive on the floor. Macy knew her friend needed urgent care, but had no way of giving it to her. The phone rang out again as she sipped some more iced coffee. Outside, nothing moved, not even the shadows.

Hurrying to her car, Macy put her bottle in the bin. She strapped herself in and drove off, the air-conditioning a welcome relief as it blew cool air over her flushed face. The hospital was only a short drive from the service centre, and she could see the turn off ahead after driving only two hundred metres.

The hospital carpark was just as deserted as the rest of town. Macy parked as close to the Emergency Room doors as she could, which was still about one hundred metres away. Once again she left her car running, glancing around unnecessarily for signs of life.

Lying on his back in front of the Emergency Room door was a man she only faintly recognised, having seen him walking around town. She had never spoken to the man, who only looked to be about eighteen, like he had just graduated high school. Ignoring him, Macy tried to get inside the hospital, but the doors were locked. Although it still worked, the intercom brought no response from inside. Macy heard the sound of it dialling whatever telephone system it was connected to.

Until it rang out, just like her phone call to Triple Zero.

Macy stepped over the man and peered inside, her hands cupped to the side of her face, touching the glass. There was no movement she could see. All quiet, just like the rest of the town.

In frustration, Macy kicked the man at her feet. He rolled slightly, before coming to rest on his back once more, his eyes closed, his expression blank.

"What the shit is happening?" Macy yelled, banging the doors of the hospital. Macy turned around, peering into the distance. A flash of movement caught her eye, a silhouette flitting through the shadows. Fear gripped her insides, pushing her breath from her lungs. From her brief glimpse, it appeared to be the same demonic form as she saw at the service station. She squinted around her, but saw nothing out of the ordinary.

The figure had disappeared.

Sweat saturated her armpits, dripped down her sides beneath her blouse, cold and shocking against the heat of the day.

Certain she was being followed, she jogged to her car, slamming the door closed. When the door was locked, she peered through her windscreen, coated in a greasy film she could never keep clean. Whatever she had seen was gone. Yet she still felt like she was being watched.

Macy drove home, travelling slower than the limit, checking for movement. She parked her car in her front yard, not caring about the crooked angle on her driveway. Flinging open her door, Macy ran inside, pressing the lock button on her remote.

When she was safely locked inside, Macy double-checked each door and window throughout the house, before moving back to the front entry. An extended look between the curtains of her front window showed no movement on the street.

Not even the little old lady on the corner was in her garden. Macy couldn't remember a morning when the old lady wasn't in her garden. Everything was the same, yet the absence of people made it completely different. While she peered through the window, Macy called every number in her phone's memory. Although it was only a small list, not one number was answered, cementing the fact that the strange happenings had moved beyond her hometown's border. Filled with sorrow, Macy wished she could call her parents, her only family she had ever known growing up. Their unexpected death two years ago still haunted her sleepless nights in the dark. She longed to hear their calming voices of reason. Macy knew they'd have a logical explanation for the day.

The sun made its way to the back of the house, while Macy stared out the window, only taking a break to visit the toilet and grab some freshly buttered toast from the kitchen.

There was a time, many months ago, when Macy's car tyre had been slashed. The following night, she had spent glued to her front window, ready to film the vandals if they returned. They had come back with a slingshot, ready to do more damage to her car. That time, it was the vehicle's rear window. That was until Macy yelled out from behind the curtains, startling them.

The pair of teenage boys, seeking revenge for an unknown misdeed, had run a few steps, turned back to where Macy stood at the window, and fired a shot straight at her. Luckily, they had hit the wooden panelling beside the window.

Macy was still rattled by that night, wondering how things would have been if they had successfully hit the window where she was. Would she have survived a rock to the head?

Today was different. Today Macy searched for an invisible foe in broad daylight; an enemy that may not even exist. And as the darkness threw its shroud on her town, Macy grew increasingly anxious. The shadows outside flirted with each other, merging into one pit of darkness where the fingers of the street light did not reach. She saw silhouetted figures dart through the dark. Macy kept her own lights off, not wanting to draw attention to herself.

Across the road, a figure opened the front door and moved inside, away from Macy's view. *Is it some kind of elaborate crime spree? A terrorist attack? Some stupid prank?* Macy wondered, dialling Triple Zero once more on her phone. The events of the day were too sinister to be a prank. Plus, surely not everyone in town would agree to such a cruel joke played on one person? There was too much effort and detail involved to be a practical joke.

Macy listened to the phone beeping loudly in her ear. There was still no answer. She grabbed her sleeping pills from the kitchen, swallowing them down with freezing cold water. She wanted nothing more than to be asleep like the rest of the town seemed to be.

Large lumbering silhouettes flitted among the shadows towards her, moving from house to house. They gathered at her front gate, which creaked slowly open. In the dim light she thought she saw a crowd of faces looking at her through the window, long sharp teeth dripping with saliva. She imagined long fingers pointing up as they whispered instructions and plans to each other. Plans to get her. As they approached the house, their feet crunched the leaves, twigs and gumnuts on her front lawn, dry and sun-bleached brown.

Macy's heartbeat increased its intensity, her stomach clamping. She raced to her bedroom, careful to tiptoe around the creaking floorboards, and hid in her closet. The figures stomped up her front stairs, as if warning her of their arrival. The thumping footsteps were like a war drum, encouraging the enemy soldiers onwards.

From her spot in her closet, Macy heard the door rattle, its noise shattering the darkness around her. Macy's body quivered, a cold sweat glued her clothes to her skin. The rattling noise stopped; Macy held her breath, listening. Waiting.

Loud banging broke the silence. A moan escaped Macy's mouth. Glass shattered, tinkling as it fell to the ground. They were in her house, her only safe place in the world. Macy's pulse pounded in her ears.

Let me fall asleep, she pleaded silently. *Why aren't you working, pills?*

She heard footsteps coming down the wooden floorboards of the hallway. It sounded like claws were scraping on the wood, heavy feet dragging them along.

The bedroom door creaked open. More scraping. The putrid stench of rotting meat wafted under the door, making Macy gag.

Macy heard a loud sniffing noise, followed by scratching at the closet door. Her own breaths were quick and shallow. She tried to be silent.

Don't open the door, she thought, a silent mantra. *Don't open the door. Don't open the door.*

Beneath the door, Macy saw two strips of darkness, blotting out the faint blue light from the moonlight filtering into the room.

The door was thrown open, slamming into the wall behind it. Macy squealed, cowering back further into the corner, as if trying to push her way through the wall. The smell consumed the wardrobe around her, stuffing itself inside.

In the darkness Macy saw a glistening body, nearly as tall as the ceiling, towering over her. Sharp teeth, almost six inches long curved down from an open mouth. Mucus dripped down its muscular body to the floor. Red eyes burned from the shadowy face.

Macy gasped, before screaming as the demonic monster began clicking, its mouth opening and closing, sniffing.

Then, as it reached out for her, Macy wished the sleeping tablets would kick in and send her to sleep one last time.

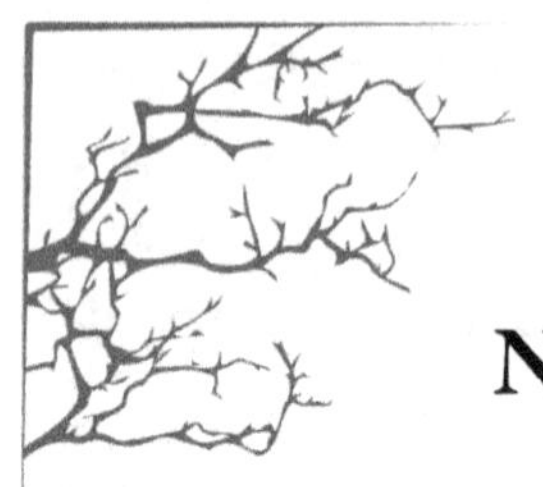

No Such Thing

Phoebe's scream sounded through the house, waking Lydia once more from her sleep. Three years into motherhood, Lydia had hoped she could finally have a night when her daughter would sleep through. Instead, she had been plagued by hundreds of nights of interrupted sleep.

Bleary-eyed, Lydia stumbled into Phoebe's room. Her night light illuminated the space, casting eerie shadows in the darkness. Phoebe stood in her cot, her hands curled tight around the railings.

"Mummy! Monster!" Phoebe cried, her eyes wide open. Tears ran down her cheeks to her gaping mouth, where a siren scream wailed into existence.

"It's okay, sweetie. Mummy's here," Lydia said gently, lifting her daughter from her cot. Toddler arms secured themselves around Lydia's neck. She could feel the tears wetting her skin. "You just had a bad dream. There's no such thing as monsters, remember."

"No, Mummy! Monster is real!" Another wail escaped Phoebe's mouth as she pointed into the closet.

"I see. So you saw the monster in your closet?" Lydia asked, attempting to quiet her daughter through empathy. *Whatever works,* she thought.

Phoebe nodded. She sniffed back her tears between sobs.

"And it opened the door and woke you up?" Lydia confirmed.

Phoebe nodded again.

"Well, Mummy is going to put you back in your cot and have a look. If he is still there I'll tell him to go away and leave you alone. How's that?" Lydia's ear drum almost exploded from the screams that followed.

"Mummy's bed!" Phoebe screamed. "I wanna go Mummy's bed!"

"I get it, sweetie. You are scared and want to join me in bed. But you sleep in here in your cot. I'm going to put you down now and check for that monster." Lydia ignored the screams and put her thrashing daughter back in her bed.

She moved over to the cupboard and opened the doors in one quick movement.

Inside, the darkness deepened into a bottomless pit of black, shadows upon shadows. The night light illuminated only the clothes and assorted knickknacks at the front of the cupboard. Lydia's eyes strained, but saw nothing out of the ordinary.

"See, Feebs? No monsters, sweetie. Remember there is no such thing. How about some warm milk and a cuddle?" Phoebe nodded her head, her screams subdued to gentle sobbing.

"Yes, pwease, Mummy." Lydia bent forward and cuddled her daughter before heading to the kitchen to prepare the milk. She had always thought it cute when Phoebe mispronounced her words.

The silence echoed through the house. Lydia was used to staying up once Phoebe had fallen asleep to catch up on housework, but after the noise of Phoebe's cries, the silence was unnerving.

When the milk was warmed, Lydia took the bottle back into Phoebe, whose eyes were struggling to remain open as she lay on her back. Her arms reached up, pulling the bottle to her lips. Phoebe drank hungrily before falling asleep. The bottle fell to her side, milk dripping slowly from the teat. Lydia picked it up and took it back to the kitchen, glad her daughter was asleep.

Once the bottle was in the fridge, Lydia turned off the lights and went back to bed. She relished the feeling of lying in her comfortable bed, surrounded by darkness. With her eyes closed, she focussed on regulating her breathing, counting as her chest rose and fell.

A scream ripped her back to reality.

"Muuummmy!" Phoebe's scream was high-pitched, digging right into Lydia's ear drum. For a moment, she thought blissfully of letting her cry it out. Motherly guilt weighed heavily on Lydia, pushing her out of bed. Her footsteps were heavy on the cool wooden floors.

"I'm here, Feebs. It's okay. Remember there's no such thing." Lydia lifted Phoebe into her arms, rocking her back and forth while singing a quiet lullaby.

Finally, when Phoebe's sobs had settled down once more, Lydia placed her back into the cot.

"Mummy. Monster in cwoset. Pwease check, Mummy?"

"I'll check again, Feebs. See? I'm moving across to the closet and opening the door," Lydia said, narrating her movements. "Now I'm looking inside. I see only your clothes and shoes. Pooo-eey, they smell," Lydia joked. Phoebe giggled timidly. "There's nothing else. There's no monsters here. There's no such thing."

Lydia closed the doors and moved back to stand next to Phoebe's cot. She looked down at her daughter, mixed feelings of love and exhaustion revolving tumultuously inside her.

"Now I'm going to lie down beside you, sweetie, okay? I'll be here if you wake up. Just reach out and hold my hand. Okay, Feebs?" Lydia said, her voice soft and soothing as she laid down on the ground. She had a pillow and a yoga mat rolled out for nights such as this, ready to fall into an uncomfortable sleep. If it meant she could sleep without worrying about rolling onto her daughter and suffocating her, then it was worth a night of discomfort.

Phoebe held on tight to Lydia's hand, her arm poking through the bars of the cot. As she drifted off to sleep, her grip relaxed, until she finally let go.

Turning onto her side, Lydia pushed her arm under the pillow and rested her head on top. She took a deep, sighing breath and closed her eyes.

The wardrobe door creaked open. Lydia watched, squinting through the soft light. A dark silhouette of a hand crept out from the door.

Lydia felt her heartbeat quicken. Her breathing became shallow as her stomach became kneaded dough. Two glistening orbs emerged from the darkness, following the hand into the room.

Jolting upright, Lydia backed toward the wall, her escape now barred. Phoebe stirred from her sleep, her eyes peering blearily at her mother.

There's no such thing as monsters, Lydia thought as the dark figure began to creep across the room. *There's no such thing.* She closed her eyes, hopeful it was just a dream. *There's no such thing.*

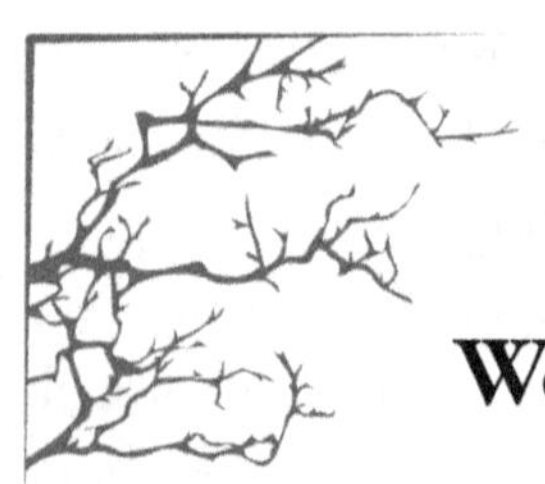

Welfare Payment

A miasma of acrid smoke filled the room. Vibrations resonated through the thick air, bringing Jonah out of his daze. After putting his beer can next to his homemade bong on the coffee table, he picked up his ringing phone.

"Shazza, babe. I thought you'd still be workin.'" Jonah's words were slurred.

"I'm on my break, Jonah... Jeez! Don't tell me you're blazing again already. It's not even lunchtime!"

Jonah looked at the clock. "Yeah, Shaz, babe, but this work-finding thing is a tough gig, yeah?" He picked up his can and slurped noisily from it.

"Oi, don't drink all the beer, Jonah! You know we don't have much left of our stash. Do you remember how difficult that was to steal? You think the gov'ment is just gonna give us more if we ask? We're at war or somethin', so save some for me, since I'm the one bringing home the bacon."

"Aww, Shaz, you're the best. I love me some bacon." Jonah licked his lips hungrily.

"No, dummy! Like, money-bacon, not real bacon. That hasn't been on the shelves for yonks! But what I meant was I make money; you don't. So I deserve some of that shit you're hoeing into!"

"I make money from me welfare cheque, Shaz. Four hunjy is in my account tomorrow." Jonah tried to make his voice smooth, but it came out husky and creepy. "I'll buy you somethin' nice."

"Not anymore, you're not! Haven't you seen the news?" Sharon's voice grew high-pitched, desperate.

"Nup, love. Been staring at the wall. No jobs in the paper, nothin' on that website you told me 'bout. Why is my money not coming?" Jonah sat upright in his chair, the fog in his head clearing a little.

"The gov'ment is cuttin' out all welfare payments until further notice. Puttin' more money into the war and shit. 'Parently you gotta get a job or join the army. What'll we do, Jonah? How will we pay rent? Shit's fucked!" Jonah could hear his girlfriend getting angry. He imagined her standing near a wall, ready to thump it.

"I'll think of somethin', Shaz. Sell our stash or some shit. I am lookin' for jobs, but nothin's available. Not for someone as dumb as dog shit like me. They want engineers, and scientists, and doctors and shit. I can't even afford a course without a job, but need a degree to get a job. What's up with that shit?" Jonah felt his heart racing, his fist clenching hard around his phone.

Through the phone he heard mumbling in the background. "Look, Jonah. Break's over. Gotta go. We'll talk at home. Love ya, babe." She smacked her lips loudly through the phone and hung up before Jonah could return the affection. He put his phone on the table and drank the last of his beer, not stopping for a breath until he was done. He scrunched up the can and threw it against the wall, where it clattered amongst a pile of old newspapers.

Then, he picked up his lighter and bong and took a long drag, breathing deeply into his lungs. He enjoyed the feeling of the marijuana blurring his memories, numbing the pain of his past. Jonah knew he wasn't the most useful person, or the smartest. School was never the right fit for him, but he just couldn't keep up with everyone else, and the teachers assumed he couldn't learn anything. So he didn't try. Hardly even opened his books, if he took them in the first place.

Every day, Jonah lived with the shame of being unemployed. He wrestled with the guilt of not bringing in money. The weed and booze helped deal with the dark thoughts. Helped keep him busy. Helped him sleep.

But it didn't give him a sense of fulfilment.

Jonah turned on the television and clicked through the channels until he found an attractive newsreader. She was giving a viewer discretionary warning. The program cut to footage of the war overseas, with soldiers being shot amidst explosions and fires. A scene showed a village of civilians helping wounded soldiers and children. Tears flowed down grief-stricken faces of parents who would never recover from the trauma of it all. It did not encourage Jonah to feel much patriotism. Instead, he was filled with disgust at the lack of humanity being shown.

Jonah put his feet up on the couch and laid down, staring at the ceiling, the sound of the news washing over him. As the drugs took effect, Jonah drifted off to sleep, the worries about his welfare payments disappearing like the smoke around him.

THE FRONT DOOR SLAMMED. Jonah woke with a start, saliva drooling down his cheek. Embarrassed, he wiped it away with his hand before transferring it to his pants.

"Jonah, where are you?" Sharon called from the hallway. Jonah heard the jangle of her keys as she took them from the door.

"In the lounge, Shaz," Jonah said. He stood up, stretched his arms above him, and moved down to greet his girlfriend.

"Have you watched the news yet, Jonah?" Sharon asked, going to the fridge and getting out a stolen beer.

Jonah nodded. "Saw a bit of it, yeah."

"It was on all the radio stations driving home." Sharon sipped her beer, before breathing out contentedly. "Shit, that's good beer. My car's nearly outta fuel, by the way. Not my day to fill up. Shoulda seen those lines though; out to the road. I'm sick of the limits we have cos of the war we don't want, but those wankers in gov'ment let happen!"

Jonah wrapped Sharon into his arms before she continued her tirade. "Nothin' we can do 'cept do our best, Love. I was thinking about what you said today, though."

"About the beer?" Sharon asked, her face crinkled with confusion as she pulled away from him.

Jonah laughed. He loved how cute she looked when she was confused. "No, Shaz. About the army or getting' a job. See, I've tried applyin' for jobs, but they want the nerd people; the ones who were good at school, or with a uni degree or whatevs, yeah? Well the other option is the army. But as I was watchin' today, those soldiers were dyin' and bein' shot and shit. I dunno how I'd go bein' away from you, on a whole other continent. But what if I was killed? Or crippled. Then it'd be even harder to find a job. Nobody will employ a cripple over a fully abled person. Not in the current state of the world anyway..." Jonah felt tears creeping into his eyes and wiped them away.

"What's worth more to me? Money or my life with you. I choose life, 'specially when it comes to fightin' for somethin' we don't agree with. Some clown in Washington wearin' makeup and playin' the big kid, like people are plastic toys. Fuck 'em, I say."

Sharon finished her beer. "What if they throw you in prison? Then you'll still be away from me and it'll all be for nothin'. It's the law now; they passed it through gov'ment. You gotta work..."

"Just 'cause it's the law, don't mean it's right, though. We don't need no bits of paper to prove we're smarter than those monkeys in Canberra or Washington. All they want is more money and power. Us pawns are pushed around and forced to do what they say. I'm not doin' it, love. They can come arrest me, or give me a job. I don't care."

"Hopefully you can find a job and we won't have to worry. I'll put in another good word for you at the shop," Sharon said.

"Thanks, Love."

"Now what are our rations givin' us to eat tonight? I hope it's not kidney beans again."

JONAH WASN'T SURE WHAT woke him at first as he stared around the bare bedroom he shared with Sharon, who had left a few hours ago for work. The room was shrouded in darkness and, as he grabbed for his phone, a loud knock pounded the front door, echoing through the house. He sat up, eyes wide open. Who would be knocking on their door, and with such urgency?

Groaning softly, Jonah pushed himself out of bed, tiptoeing through the house on bare feet, remaining as quiet as possible. He didn't recall owing anyone money, but he wasn't organised with these things. They had only bought the basic rations this week, so had nothing much to steal. *Even though a thief wouldn't be knocking loudly*, Jonah thought. Peeking through the front curtains, he saw a police car, its lights flashing. Two burly officers stood at the front door, peering at their watches and looking around them. With some hand signals, one officer moved to the back of the house, unimpeded by gates or fences.

"Mister Holland, open the door, please!" The officer knocked at the door as they spoke loudly, one hand on his holstered weapon. His arm muscles tensed, bulging beneath the skin of his thick arms.

Jonah's first impulse was to remain standing there, not moving as he watched the police officers walk back to their car and drive away. At least he hoped that's what they'd do. But what then? What happened when they left and came back with reinforcements? Or came back when Sharon was home and she opened the door? At least they'd been able to finish the drugs and alcohol, so they had no banned substances on the property.

This had to be due to his lack of success at finding paid work. Maybe they'd take him to a job vacancy, or straight to the army recruitment office. Jonah doubted that.

After the number of letters he had ignored, hoping in vain to find a job before the cut-off date. It had never happened, and Jonah felt an overwhelming sense of failure, as if his life held no value. Those letters had joined his dignity in the bin.

The policeman picked up his radio and muttered something Jonah could not catch. It beeped in return, followed by unintelligible chatter. As he watched the policeman at the front door reply, Jonah noticed a swarm of police officers in full riot gear swamp the front yard. There must have been at least ten officers, shields held before them as they moved towards the house. Two officers held a large black cylinder between them. Four officers broke from the group and moved quickly round the back. A police van pulled in on the road behind them.

Jonah had forgotten the officer at the back. Jonah was out of his line of sight, but he was now stuck in the front bedroom, used for storage of old clothes and stuff they never used. Looking back through the window, Jonah saw the police begin to slam the black cylinder into his front door. Other officers fanned out behind them, guns ready to fire. The door thumped as the ram slammed into it, making Jonah jolt in his spot.

The officers slammed the door again successfully, the door slamming back against the wall as they hustled in. Jonah backed against the wall, his hands in the air. The armed officers stormed into the room, their guns pointed at Jonah, yelling directions at him, a cacophony of almost indecipherable shouts.

Once he had dropped to the ground, his arms splayed out beside him, his nose pressed to the carpet, Jonah heard the officers rush in. The carpet smelled musty, like dusty dirt beginning to mould. His arms were brought painfully behind his back, the cuffs cutting deep into his wrists. Then the officers pulled him quickly to his feet, making him stumble. He was led out to the police van, where a number of other men waited cuffed and morose. An officer unlocked one hand and brought it to the front of his body, before locking them together once more.

Jonah sat squashed between two larger blokes, who both smelled like a dumpster that hadn't been emptied for weeks. Staring out the window, Jonah wished nothing more than to speak with Sharon, hoping she would be told where he was. He watched the city go past as they were driven to the police station. Jonah had obviously been the last arrest for this load.

At the station, the men were herded from the van, through a door that looked as if it would survive a nuclear blast, and into a large jail cell with about twenty other men. Jonah licked his large lips as he shuffled into the cell, still handcuffed. He noticed that every inmate was still wearing cuffs. Each man looked different, but they all had one thing in common: they all looked unemployed.

Their hair was uncut, unkempt. Their clothes were ragged, with various stains and rips. Their faces were mostly unshaved. Eyes were devoid of hope.

Some of them were pacing the ground, peering out at the police officers who were either working at computers, or watching them, laughing.

Jonah sat next to two inmates who were deep in a whispered conversation. He heard wisps of their conversation as their hushed words scrambled to be heard.

"I heard that when they get taken away, they don't get no second chance," one man said, looking around him. "I seen one man hit on the head before. Seen it with me own eyes."

"My mate Johnno reckoned that people were disappearing from the country. They'd get arrested, then never heard from again. Not in the army or anything, though. Oh no. See, the government is tryna save money, see? And how do you do that with everyone thrown in jail? Can't, see?" The man leaned closer to the other. "See, I heard they get killed and minced up to feed the troops overseas."

The other man gasped, his mouth agape. "Bullshit! You didn't hear that shit!"

"Swear on me life, I did hear it. Where else would they go, except for food?" He leaned back, his hands held clasped on his lap.

"I dunno, hey. If it's true and they do get killed, then maybe they're used for fertiliser or something? Fuckin' blended up like a hipster smoothie, or some shit. Help the farmers grow food? Aren't they in a draft or something?"

"You mean a drought? Yeah, mate. No rain, see? I was out woop-woop a few years back. Knew a bloke out Birdsville way, see? Well, while I was there, I seen not one drop of rain. Not a drop of amber ale out that way since the war, either. Just tasteless Adam's ale, shipped in on trucks... or is it trucked in on trucks? Whatever, they brung it into town in a big truck."

Jonah sat back, deep in thought. What if it was true? What if the government were killing unemployed people to save resources? Were they even allowed to do that?

The door was unlocked and opened noisily, a metallic clang stopping the conversations around the room. A policeman with a completely shaved head stood, staring at a clipboard.

"Liam Jackson and Rodney Bullock. You're up! Follow me, men!" The officer stood, looking impatient as he frowned around the room. The man next to Jonah, who had been in conversation stood up and looked at his friend.

"Guess I'll know what happens soon. Nice knowin' ya, mate." He began walking away, his cuffed hands drifting awkwardly from side to side.

Jonah stood and paced the room, staring at the floor, only glancing up if he saw a pair of feet in front of him. He wanted to speak with Sharon, sure she would be freaking out at his absence. It felt like he had been in jail for hours.

Finally he worked up the courage to go to the side of the cell and call out to the closest officer. "'Scuse me, mate. Do I get my phone call? Need to call the missus."

The female officer sitting closest to him looked up from her computer, staring straight at him. "What did you say?"

"I asked if I could call me missus. I don't even know if she knows where I am," Jonah replied, smiling as pleasantly as he could.

There was a moment of silence where the officer looked like she was trying to process his request, before she started guffawing as if he had said the world's funniest joke. He sat back down, his face burning hot. He felt some of the fellow inmates staring pitifully at him, as if he wasn't the first to have asked.

Finally, after what seemed like another few hours, Jonah's name was called. The cell had emptied somewhat since he had first arrived, with only a slow trickle of newcomers being thrown in. Jonah stood up and followed the bald officer along a winding hall. Their footsteps echoed down the corridor, past closed doorways, disappearing into nothingness.

The hallway opened into a large room the size of a concert hall. Large metallic machines filled the space, whirring noisily as they worked doing whatever they had been invented for. Jonah was certain he would find out soon enough. He was led up a set of metal stairs, and when he reached the top he knew what the machines were for.

His stomach whirled inside him as he dry-retched. If he had eaten earlier, Jonah would have vomited. Sweat beaded on his forehead, his heartrate quickening. If he wasn't cuffed, he would have wiped his sweaty palms on his shorts.

Jonah stared into the large metal vat beneath him, where a blade spun round quickly, mixing a red liquid. The officer pulled out a key and unlocked the handcuffs. Jonah rubbed his wrists, working out the pain mindlessly, staring into the mixture below. He realised his hands were shaking.

"Here's your last stop, criminal," the officer announced, stepping back. "Consider it your welfare payment. Try to avoid the blades." He began laughing as Jonah felt hands upon his back.

Jonah tried resisting, pushing back against the force, but he was tired, hungry and weak. Another officer joined in and, as he fell forward, Jonah wished he could see Sharon one last time; he hoped she wouldn't lose her job.

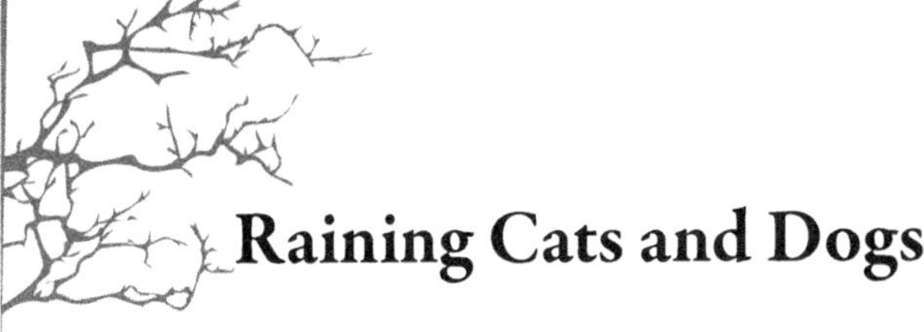

Raining Cats and Dogs

"It's raining dogs and cats out there!" Kane exclaimed as he looked out the window. He turned to his partner Levi, who looked up from reading the newspaper.

"You know I love you, Kane, but sometimes I hate when you say your silly little sayings. Not to mention you said it wrong. Why can't you just say it's raining heavily?"

"It's called an idiot, darling," Kane said, walking to Levi.

"Idiom," Levi muttered.

"What?" Kane said.

"It's called an idiom."

Kane threw his arms around Levi's shoulders, kissing his hair as he leaned down. Levi leaned his head back and planted a kiss on Kane's lips, enjoying the rough bit of stubble.

A loud thumping on the roof broke them apart, Levi standing up next to Kane. Both men looked up at the ceiling, the thumping continuing.

The men rushed to the window and looked out, their jaws hanging open.

Outside the house, dead animals—dogs and cats—littered the wet ground. Their corpses were piled up, lifeless.

"Fucking impossible!" exclaimed Levi. "Since when have animals fell from the fucking sky?"

"Maybe it's some kind of tornado?" Kane suggested. "Or a plane had its cargo doors open?" His voice quivered as he stared out the window, motionless.

"You did this!" Levi said, his voice accusing.

"How could I fucking make cats and dogs fall from the sky?" Kane yelled, taking a step back.

"You said it was raining cats and dogs, and now it literally is raining cats and bloody dogs!"

"What, so now I'm psychic or something? Rainman or... or Harvey Bloody Potter?"

"It's Harry Potter! We've been together for three years now, and you don't even know my favourite fucking book series character. Some boyfriend you are..." Levi shook his head, exasperated.

"You knew I wasn't smart when we first shagged and you were okay to stay with me. You love my body, not my brains," Kane said, attempting to placate things. "I'm sorry, darling."

"I forgive you, but I'm still making you re-watch all the movies this weekend."

"Deal. But how about we deal with this... thing outside? What would Harry Potter do? Is there some spell to make it go away? *Woof-gardium Levi-meow-sa?*"

"Don't do that. Don't you make fun of it!" Levi's face was one big warning sign.

Together they moved back to the window, staring out as the animals continued to fall from the sky, small mountains of bloody, matted fur.

"There's too many out there to be an aeroplane collision," Levi said. "Let's look out the front and see if it's any different." They held hands as they walked to the front of the house. There was no difference in weather out the front.

"Maybe your storm idea is correct," Levi said. "Though it seems like a massive coincidence to believe. You and your bloody sayings." Levi smiled, a peace offering.

"Surely it isn't magic though. Magic isn't real. *Is it*?" Kane's face screwed up as he peered out the window.

"Well I guess you've let the cat out of the bag now, Kane," Levi joked. "How about we let sleeping dogs lie?"

"But they're dead, not sleeping," Kane said, not understanding the joke.

"I'm trying to use one of your idioms. Look, forget it. Let's turn on the TV and see if there's any news about it," Levi said, moving to the lounge. When he turned on the television there was no signal.

"Damn cats must have ruined the aerial!" Levi said.

"Don't forget about the dogs," Kane added. Levi glared at him in reply. "Sorry, darls."

At that moment, a loud bang reverberated through the air from outside, the power also going out.

"Power's out," Kane said, looking around at the appliances.

"No shit, Sherlock!"

"Now who's using an idiom?" Kane muttered.

"Are you sure you don't mean idiot?" Levi felt his heart quicken as he tried to bring his anger under control. When it came to situations out of his control and comfort zone, Levi turned to anger to feel normal again. It was something he had been working on with his therapist. He took his breaths and counted to ten before continuing.

"Look, I'm sorry. It's just so strange to have animals falling from the sky, and I'm scared. We were expecting a summer storm, but this is ridiculous. Surely I'm dreaming." Levi looked at his phone, which had no signal.

"Anything?" Kane asked. "I've got nothing." He held up his phone as if Levi might have thought he was lying.

"Me neither. Looks like these stupid things outside have cut off power and communication lines. Wi-Fi doesn't even work without electricity."

The thumping on the roof subsided, making Kane and Levi look up at the ceiling.

"Seems like it's stopping," Kane said. "Want to go outside and check things out?"

"That could be pretty dangerous, Kane. What if they're full of disease?" Levi said, peering warily out the window.

"The neighbours are out there too. Maybe they know what's happening?" Kane said, beginning to unlock the front door. He took a step outside, and quickly poked his head back in. "I hope they hurry up with the electricity. It's as hot as an oven out here." He grabbed a hat and went outside, waving to their neighbour.

Levi hesitated, watching Kane through the window. The weather did seem warm. Much hotter than usual. He felt the sweat bead on his skin as he made his way into the thermometer in the kitchen.

"Fuck me," he muttered as he saw the digital temperature reading on the display. "Forty-eight fucking degrees! And it's not even Christmas yet!" He looked out the kitchen window, his clothes soaked through, sticking to his body. The sun blazed down on the animal corpses in the backyard, heat emanating through the glass. Levi glanced back at the thermometer, which now showed a reading of fifty-nine degrees. Rushing to the front window, thermometer still in hand, Levi looked out to Kane, who was nowhere in sight.

Feeling faint, Levi moved to the front door, where Kane had made a path through the corpses. About halfway down the path, Kane laid across a number of dead animals, his skin red and burnt. Kane was as lifeless as the animal bodies around him, one arm thrown across his eyes.

Levi glanced at the thermometer, which now flashed seventy-seven degrees, the numbers increasing every few seconds. As he collapsed to the floor, the memory of Kane's last words echoed through Levi's brain: "It's as hot as an oven out here."

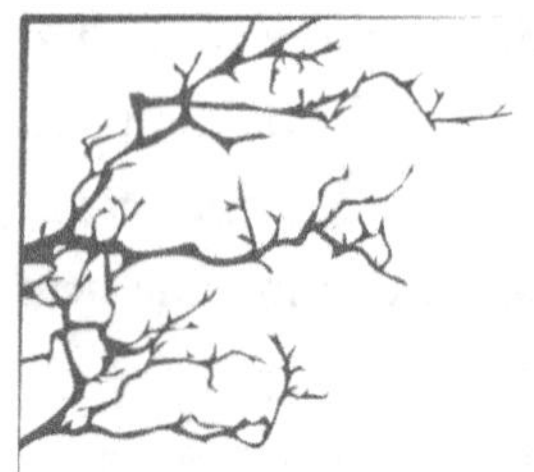

Fire Escape

The alarm blared, pounding in Neil's ears. He pushed himself up to a sitting position and wiped the sleep from his eyes.

"Evacuate! Evacuate!" a robotic voice called between the klaxon sounds.

"Light on," he called. The room remained shrouded in complete darkness. "Light on."

If it wasn't for the red flashing light on the ceiling, he would have assumed he had gone blind, something his glasses wouldn't correct. He reached out and put them on before flicking the manual light switch beside his bed.

Still the room remained in darkness. He gave it a few extra test clicks but to no avail. Outside his door, Neil heard muffled shouts and the pattering of hurried footsteps, feeling a pang of jealousy. He had never spoken to his neighbours and felt a wave of regret. Did they even know he was still in here?

"Siri, what time is it?" he called into the void, knowing his phone always had answers. The siren remained the only sound in the room. "What the hell is happening?"

Picking up his phone, he saw it was just past midnight and he had no reception. Typical. His plan was the cheapest he could afford on his minimum wage as a computer technician, and the building's internet was out. The alarm must be connected to the solar backup battery, generating only enough energy to alert the thousands of people shoved into the building.

After dragging his lifeless legs to the edge of the bed, Neil pulled his wheelchair closer to him. With a grunt of effort, he heaved himself into the chair, put his phone and wallet in his lap and wheeled himself to the front door, veering around his weights set, using his mind's map. At the door, he looked pointlessly around his dark studio apartment for his important stuff, but with the siren continuing to sound, he felt pressure to leave. He opened the door to a wall of smoke. Small emergency lights struggled to illuminate the billowing dark clouds filling the corridor.

Neil coughed as the door began to swing closed behind him. With a spark of ingenuity, he stopped it from closing with his arm and moved back inside, heading to his kitchenette. Grabbing his two clean hand towels, he wet them before tying them around his head, making sure they covered his mouth. They smelled like his musty drawers, but they'd offer some protection for his lungs against the smoke outside.

He emerged once more, this time feeling more prepared. The door clicked shut, quietly ominous among the sirens. The absence of an orange tinge was a good sign: the fire was not on his floor.

Yet.

The exit was on the ground level; he needed to get down to escape. He began to move towards the lift only to realise it wouldn't be working without power. And even if it was, would it be safe to lock himself into a metal box as it descended slowly, possibly through fire?

But what other way was there? For able-bodied people, there were stairs. Nice and easy, one step at a time. Neil knew that if he took the stairs, he'd probably need to leave his chair behind. His beloved wheelchair.

Yes, he was bound to his chair, but the freedom it gave him was irreplaceable. It allowed him to go wherever he wanted to.

Except up and down stairs.

They were able to invent a way for people to live underwater. They'd made holograms possible. Hell, they'd even created robots that could complete complicated heart surgery.

But they'd never bothered to give people with a disability more mobility. There was no money in it, he guessed, and money made the world go round. Money had also increased the rising sea levels from global warming, not that governments were any closer to acknowledging its existence. For three centuries now scientists had predicted the water below, lapping at the lower levels of the building he lived in, and those all around the city. At least they were luckier than Venice, which was now unliveable, its inhabitants evicted with no home address. Refugees in their own country.

Warmth emanated through the stairwell door's white painted wood. Every set of steps felt like another place he wasn't invited to as if they were purposely built to keep him out. These steps led to his freedom; these steps prevented him from freedom.

Perhaps someone will come along to help me downstairs, he thought as he opened the door. The smoke glowed orange upstairs, sending heat rushing downwards. His submersible craft waited in the garage below but he needed his wheelchair to work the machine, or he'd have nowhere to sit.

The sudden sound of silence echoed around him, leaving only the crackling of the fire to taunt his ears.

Sweat beaded his forehead as he thought about his descent. His breath was humid beneath the towels, a hint of smoke sneaking in to steal the fresh air. Glancing up, he saw the dancing fingers of flame make their way into the stairwell, consuming the door and cracking the concrete. It was only a matter of time before it made its way downstairs to him. He felt like a sitting duck; he needed to act.

Building up courage, he decided on his plan. He would have to push his beloved chair downstairs and drag himself along the railings. It would be heavy work with just his arms, but he knew he was strong. Was he strong enough to descend three storeys?

There was only one way to find out.

He held on to the railing, pulling himself forward and down to the ground, his chair wobbling beneath him. Once he was sprawled on the smooth concrete, Neil grabbed his chair by the frame, pausing as if he was listening to it whisper to him. If he wanted to be independent when—if—he got downstairs, then he needed to risk rolling his chair down the steps.

Above him, Neil heard a loud cracking noise and, as he looked up through the orange haze, he thought he saw long fissures appear in the concrete. He needed to move quickly.

With a grunt, he pushed his chair forward, grimacing as it bounced over the steps and rolled onto its side as it hit the landing below. Reaching out, he gripped the metal balustrade, the heat beginning to flow through the metal. It wasn't burning hot yet, but it was warmer than his morning cup of coffee. He began to pull himself downwards, hand over hand, his legs trailing uselessly behind him. The chair lying lifeless, waiting patiently for him, encouraged him on.

Neil coughed. The towels had begun to dry out in the heat, allowing smoke to push through to his parched mouth. He licked his lips, but they remained dry. The building rumbled around him, whether from the heat breaking it apart or some kind of explosion, he didn't know. He focussed only on dragging himself to safety.

When he had struggled to the first landing, he lifted his chair back onto its wheels and pushed it down once more, following it as he had before. The heat was increasing, the orange glow becoming fiercer as the fire spread above. He felt his lungs wheezing as they fought to breathe.

Somehow, he made it to the last landing before he felt like giving up. His body had become saturated with sweat; his glasses were smudged and dirty, making it hard to see; his breathing had become shallow and raspy; his arms ached from overuse. When he had pushed his chair to the hallway below—the hallway to the garage of freedom—he felt like that exertion had drained all his energy. The metal railings had burned his hand, blisters forming among the red skin.

Flames were now licking the ceiling above, like fingers scrabbling to lift the roof. The heat reminded him of his old outback town, now vacant, everybody agreeing the temperature had become unbearable year-round. Tears mingled with the sweat on his cheeks. Whether he was crying due to the smoke, the pain in his burnt hands, or the haunting memories of his youth, he wasn't sure. Perhaps it was all his pain and suffering melting together. The fire burning around him juxtaposed the dying embers of desire within him. He wanted nothing more than to lie down and let the fire consume him, as it had his crumbling home.

One particular memory clamoured for his attention. He had been about fifteen and had broken down, a crying mess of despair. His mother had attempted to placate him, with minimal success.

"What's the matter, Neil?" she had asked, embracing him in her arms.

"People always stare at me. I feel like some kind of circus freak!" His tears flowed freely, releasing the pent-up frustration he had been holding in. "I feel like they're judging me. Walking around with their perfect legs. I'm sick of it!"

His mother had told him that yes, he was different. And yes, people stared.

"Who doesn't stare at things they're not used to?" she had whispered into his hair. "But we also stare at the beautiful things in life, like sunrises or art. You, my wonderful Neil, are beautiful. Your chair gives you different abilities. You'll never get tired of standing up, for one. You're not going to hit your head on things like I always do. Your story will always be different from others, and that will make you incredibly intriguing to people. I think you're perfect. I love you forever and always." Neil had smiled through his tears and, although he knew his mother would love him no matter what, there was a lot of truth in what she had said.

Since then, he had appreciated the beauty of uniqueness.

As the flames crackled around him, he felt the same sense of despair as he had then. His mother would be devastated if he was to die in the fire. He knew she would be cheering him on like it was a game of basketball he'd played as a kid.

With a sudden burst of energy, he reached out to the banister and pulled himself to his waiting chair, coughing up phlegm as he dragged himself down. When he reached the landing, he righted his chair once more and used the hot railing to help pull him into his seat. His burnt hands screamed in pain as they rubbed against scorching surfaces.

With one last burst of adrenaline-fuelled energy, Neil pushed his chair along the hallway, through the smoke, until he reached the clean air of the open garage. Waves lapped at the building's foundations. A grey haze wafted along the water until it dispersed, replaced by cleaner air.

The garage was mostly empty when he moved through the door. He assumed most people had driven their vehicles to safety. Slight ripples waved through the murky water, debris and rubbish floating listlessly. He moved along the metal catwalk to the ramp where his own specially-built vehicle bobbed, waiting for action.

As he wheeled himself into his submersible vehicle and started the engine, Neil couldn't wait to see his mother. He had one incredibly unique story to tell her.

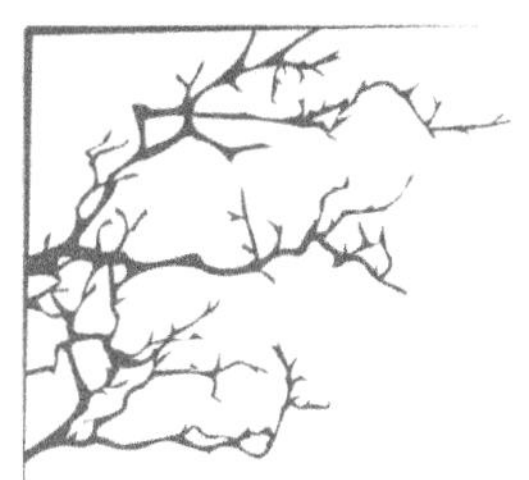

Armalina

Armalina looked at the smouldering debris of her home. Somewhere beneath the glowing ash was her family, dead. Father, mother, sister; all gone forever. Her eyes burned as she looked on, wet with tears; from sadness or the smoke, she wasn't sure. The land around her was scorched, black beneath the bright sunlight.

From her small copse in the forest she had watched—feeling utterly helpless—as dragons ravaged her home, a place she had lived all of her eighteen years. So many memories lived within the charred skeleton of her home, now living only in her mind. Of the many spells she knew, none of them could repair the damage in front of her.

She kicked the remnants of her destroyed home, relishing the feeling of heat through her leather boots. Even though it hurt, it was a distraction from the pain of losing her family. Before today, life had been good; she thought she had it all.

And now she had nothing.

No family. No home.

Only the scorched heap behind her. Moving to her pile, she took stock of her belongings: a dagger in its sheath, a half-full water skin, two rabbits and a snare. Plus the few spells she knew.

Not much, but enough to survive. Wiping away her tears, Armalina walked away, leaving her old world behind. A new world lay through the dark woods in front of her. If she didn't leave now, she would stay there forever, hoping the ghosts of her past would materialise into being.

Her father had regaled her with tales of large kingdoms while he whittled the wood he lopped into useful items. Furniture, crockery, toys, and the occasional sculpture. Armalina loved her dad's stories, filled with an infectious energy.

This destruction was exactly what her father was trying to avoid, choosing to live with his family in a life of solitude, away from scheming nobles, prying peasants and bloodthirsty vagabonds. A life away from his previous position in the king's army.

If anyone came to cause them trouble, her family had their magic spells and her father's skill with weapons to ward them off. Each weapon was carefully sharpened each day.

It hadn't worked to stop dragons. The creatures hadn't been known in the world for centuries, and had become a distant myth. Until they had rained from the sky in a shower of fire and stone, razing her home. Their descent had rumbled the ground, like thunder in a summer storm, vibrations rattling every molecule of their bodies. Their house had shivered, as if the rain of fiery dragon eggs were freezing cold.

She sobbed as she thought of Isalina, her sister, who had perished. The roars of the dragons had devoured all other sound, and Armalina wondered—hoped—her family hadn't suffered. She imagined their final moments, horror hammering her chest. Visions of them cowering together, burning as they screamed in pain. What had they been thinking in their final moments? Had they suffered, or was their death mercifully quick?

Her home was nestled in a large clearing of the forest, a small but swift-flowing creek provided water. They had kept a garden to grow fruit and vegetables, enough for their family.

All that was left now was a dry creek bed and burnt vegetation. No extra food to fill her belly on the journey.

Her father had shown her the direction of the kingdom of Emilica, so she knew the general course she needed to head.

Without having seen a map, she couldn't be sure if she was heading the right way, instead needing to rely on instinct and natural pathways.

Night began to fall as she traipsed through the forest, shadows growing longer, darker. Her mood matched the murky darkness around her. Armalina had never been in the forest at night-time without her father, and even then, they had not travelled more than one hundred metres or so through the trees. There were too many dangerous creatures lurking to eat unsuspecting prey.

Armalina didn't want to be that prey.

Daytime wasn't much safer, though at least she could see around her.

Her mother had taught her the spells she had learned in her youth as an apprentice witch, but they were few and nowhere near enough to guarantee her safety.

Her mother had only been taught domestic spells to help her become a good little wife, but not much more. Armalina knew spells that could light a fire, clean a house, entrance an animal to kill for food, or help their garden grow. She was sure there were more spells to learn, but she knew nothing of their existence.

Her mother had tried to teach her potions, but she could never master the art. Following instructions was not her strong suit. Isalina was the potions prodigy, and had learned their mother's potion recipe book by heart. Armalina was sure she had heard her sister reciting potion recipes in her sleep, late at night when she lay restless, listening to the forest's night noises around them.

The moon's soft light dappled through the canopy of trees, white fingers searching through the darkness, unable to bring much more than a dim illumination to the path ahead of Armalina. She could hear animals moving about around her, shrieks and calls sharing secrets she could not decipher.

There were unspeakable monsters hiding from view, waiting for full darkness to make their move. Armalina's father had told her stories of the Dathgol, described them in detail to prevent her from exploring further in the forests.

The Dathgol's long fingers ending in sharp claws had always chilled Armalina, and she always shivered like her back was being stroked. Thin lips barely covered their razor sharp teeth, a forked tongue tasting the air as it flicked out like a snake's. It towered over humans, as tall as a house, staring with orange eyes that lit up in the darkness. Translucent skin stretched tight over their bodies, covered in coarse hair, rough enough to graze skin into a bloody pulp.

No, she hoped she wouldn't come face to ugly face with a Dathgol.

The Achlonakai were not much better. With bodies like a large tiger, and the head of a dog, they were fearsome beasts. Their ability to think and talk made them incredibly clever, travelling in packs to help them hunt. One Achlonakel could slaughter a grown man in ten seconds. If it chose to, of course. Together, they were ruthless.

Armalina came to a clearing, the moon shimmering on the dew-tipped grass. Clouds rolled slowly across the sky, glowing as it approached the moon and bringing dark patches to the world below. Her eyes were heavy and burdened with tiredness, and she felt sluggish. Alone and lost, she stopped to make camp, looking around for immediate danger. Apart from the animal noises that had become part of the background, Armalina could neither see nor hear anything of interest. After weighing up her options, she decided to light a fire, wanting to ward off the cold. She hoped it wouldn't attract any dangerous creatures to her. With only her dagger, spells and fighting spirit, she would find it difficult to fight them off.

She gathered some twigs and bracken from the ground nearby, piling them up in the centre of the clearing.

"Lithueen hothuam," she muttered, touching the sticks gently with her fingers. A small fire jumped from the sticks. She took a step back, letting the smoke rise from the crackling wood. Warmth made its way towards her, seeping through her cold clothes.

As the flames built, she prepared the rabbit she had caught, gutting it and placing it on a makeshift spit.

When the fire was hot enough, she placed the rabbit above the coals and waited for it to cook. She sipped the last of her water, enjoying the feeling as the cool liquid soothed her dry throat. She would need to find more tomorrow.

The fire brought unhappy memories of her family's murder inside their home and, wiping away tears, she stared into the fire, allowing it to consume her thoughts.

A snapping twig outside the clearing broke her away from her thoughts, and she peered into the darkness. She thought she could see a multitude of eyes peering out at her, and she shivered, feeling her pulse quicken. Her hand moved to the hilt of her dagger, ready to bring it out at a moment's notice.

Dark clouds filled the sky above, shrouding the stars and moon. The eyes remained, blinking, staring. Unnerving. As long as they stayed there out of sight, Armalina would be content.

The smell of the rabbit cooking made her stomach clench with hunger. Its juices hissed as they fell to the hot wood beneath.

Deciding she could wait no longer, Armalina removed the rabbit from the fire, burning her fingertips. She gasped as the oil burned her mouth, but continued to swallow her first mouthful. Although the meat was tough and chewy, it was enough to put a dent on her hunger and stop the pangs. Had she been at home, the rabbit would have been prepared with herbs and fresh vegetables, cooked slowly to tenderise the meat. The skin would have been useful to make clothes; instead it was wasted.

Burnt, like her family and home.

She felt a huge gaping cavern in her chest, like invisible hands had reached in and wrenched out her insides. Her body ached and she was tired. Overwhelmingly tired.

Cracking twigs approaching the clearing made Armalina stop chewing her last mouthful, wiping her mouth with her sleeve as she peered into the darkness. Again, her hand moved instinctively to the hilt of her dagger. A hulking silhouette crept from behind a tree, moving slowly towards Armalina. She stood up, drawing out her dagger and holding it in front of her. A quick glance around her showed no other movement in the clearing.

Focussing back on the approaching figure, she called out. "Who are you? Declare yourself!" Armalina tried to keep her voice steady and firm, but she heard a small tremble that matched her outstretched arm.

The figure remained silent, continued moving closer.

"Who are you? Declare yourself or I will be forced to attack." The tremble was still there, encouraged by her ragged breaths.

The figure stopped, as if it was staring.

Continuing forwards, it cackled before speaking, its voice high and croaky. "Don't worry, child. I am but an old man travelling through the forest." He came into view and Armalina looked, sizing him up. He wore a traveller's cloak, with shaggy, unkempt hair flowing out above the collar. A long beard showered down his chest. His eyes glittered from the shadows of his cloak.

"I saw you by the fire and watched. I wanted to be sure, doubly sure, that you were friendly." He smiled, revealing gaps in his teeth. "I could see and smell something tasty, and wanted to join you for my evening meal."

"But I have nothing le—" Armalina began.

"Nonsense. I can see you have no more food. I was going to offer you some of my provisions," the man croaked, standing on the opposite side of the fire. "I don't have much, but you're welcome to share."

He reached into a satchel hanging on his back and pulled out some dried meat, two apples, and a loaf of bread.

Armalina watched warily. Her father had warned them about accepting anything from strangers who might happen to pass through, especially food.

But the rabbit had been small and she was hungry. Surely an apple couldn't hurt.

"Thank you," she said, reaching out for an apple. She raised it to her nose. It smelt normal and, as she bit into the crunchy flesh, juices ran down her chin. "Where are you headed anyway?" she asked the man.

"Away from the dragons, of course! Far away. I saw them fighting over yonder." He gave a half-hearted wave. "And you. I sense some sadness in you, young'un. Dragons been plaguin' you, too?"

Armalina sighed, staring at the crackling fire. Would it hurt to tell this man—this stranger—what had happened to her family? Would that make her look more vulnerable? Or more like a woman with nothing left to lose?

She needed help, but could she trust this man?

"A dragon destroyed my home and family. I'm off to seek vengeance. Any dragon that I see will feel my wrath," Armalina said, deciding the truth would be less complicated. Although she still didn't trust the man, he had shared some food with her, even though she would only accept the apple. What animal had the jerky been made from?

The man chuckled. He drank from his bottle, rivulets of liquid running down his beard.

"Now that's a fight I'd enjoy seeing," he said between cackles. "I'm sorry, lovey, but I would put my gold on the dragon to win." He saw Armalina's glare. "No offence. But if that dagger is all you have, then it won't be much help against a dragon. Tell me, did you see the dragon that destroyed your home and family?"

She nodded grimly. "Yes. I saw each claw the size of daggers. Each tooth in a mouth that spewed fire. Each wing as it beat gales to fan the fire. I know all about the power of the dragon I saw. But maybe I'm more powerful than I appear. That dragon should fear me," she added, bravado lining her words. She didn't feel as courageous as she said she was.

"Good on you," the man said, condescending. "That might be... if there were just one dragon. I counted four beasts before I left."

He paused, chewing on a strip of meat, the sound of the fire embracing them. "But best of luck all the same."

Armalina yawned, sleep beginning to wash powerfully over her. She couldn't sleep, not with the man close by. Her father had warned her about moments like these. What men were capable of doing.

"Perhaps you should get some sleep. You'll need to be well-rested if you're to fight those dragons," the man said. "I will stay awake some more and watch this fire die into embers. I'm usually late to bed, mind. I can add some wood before I turn in."

Armalina lay down near the fire, her head resting on an outstretched arm. She watched the flames jumping through heavy-lidded eyes, beginning to dream of quenching the fire from the dragons forever.

She had just dozed off when she startled awake, fear gripping her body. Something wasn't right. The fire had died to glowing embers.

The stench of rotting meat and human waste made her crinkle her nose. Jolting upright she searched the clearing. The man had moved from his position. Where was he?

Armalina stood up and swivelled around, reaching for her dagger.

It was gone!

"Looking for this, lovey?" a deep voice asked, sing-song and taunting. The cloak lay crumpled in the grass and, instead of the hunched figure of the man, stood a towering body of terror. It seemed to be as tall as the trees around them.

A Dathgol.

Her dagger was held between long fingers, their claws the size of the dagger itself. Armalina froze in fear, unable to take her eyes off the Dathgol's own orange ones, as if they reflected the embers of the dying fire. A tail whipped through the air behind it, like a cat's.

Coming to her senses, Armalina glanced around, searching for an escape route.

"There's no use trying to run, girl," the Dathgol rasped. "I will catch you in an instant, though I would enjoy the brief moment of exercise." It began to laugh and threw the dagger into the woods behind it.

It was so close now, bending forwards, stiletto teeth protruding from its thin lips. The Dathgol was close enough to see the dark lines of its blood pulsing beneath its translucent skin. Armalina took a step back, before remembering the spell she used to stun larger animals to kill.

In the past she had only ever used it on deer and one cow. She had no idea whether it worked on creatures of evil like the Dathgol.

But she had to try. It was all she had left to defend herself. She didn't think she had much time.

Staring at the Dathgol, she whispered: "Starum bladius."

It continued bending forward, the cloying stench making her feel sick, her stomach roiling within her.

"Starum bladius!" Her voice trembled.

Its fingers now began to stroke her hair, her clothes. She shivered like she had when her father had told her tales in her youth.

The thought of her father gave her courage, steeling her muscles.

She tried again, putting her energy into imagining the Dathgol as a statue. Its mouth was open above her, hot breath blowing down from between rows of sharp teeth.

"Starum bladius!" Her voice was loud and clear as she held her hands out above her, palms facing away.

The Dathgol stopped moving. Its breaths were soft, like a night breeze in the spring, though it still reeked.

For a few seconds, Armalina was also stunned, surprised the spell had worked. She wished her father had told her the Dathgol were shapeshifters. Perhaps he didn't know.

Perhaps nobody had managed to make it away from one alive.

The Dathgol in front of her began to move its fingers, wriggling them as if only just learning how to control them. Those burning orange eyes stared beading down at her, unblinking, focussed only on Armalina.

She needed that dagger before the spell wore off. There was no way she would be able to outrun the Dathgol. Armalina's mother had taught her what she had named "the lazy spell", which could summon a nearby object into her hands. Armalina had only ever practised in the kitchen when she had forgotten to pick something from the garden. There was no use wasting magic when you had the use of arms and legs. It was a difficult spell to master, mainly due to lack of practice, but eventually she had made it work.

She needed it to work now.

Ignoring the moving Dathgol in front of her, Armalina concentrated on the dagger her father had given her to help her hunt.

With arms held out towards the forest, she chanted the spell, hoping to get the pronunciation correct. "Fyndamuth steffendo dagger. Fyndamuth steffendo dagger. She heard a rustle in the leaf litter of the forest floor.

Whether it was her dagger moving or some kind of creature, she wasn't sure.

The Dathgol moved its arms, reaching out towards Armalina.

"Fyndamuth steffendo dagger. Fyndamuth steffendo dagger!" There was a whistling sound as the dagger came flying towards her.

Faith in her magical ability kept her steady and unflinching, the hilt slapping the palm of her hand.

As quickly as she could, Armalina slashed at the Dathgol's arms, cutting them above the elbow. They fell to the ground where they wriggled like senseless snakes in the dim light. The claws dug into the ground, inching towards her.

Grunting with exertion, she slashed at the spindly legs, the torso dropping into a puddle of dark slush, more liquid spurting from its wounds. It gave a high-pitched squeal that made Armalina's muscles contract, her jaw clenched. Resisting the urge to cover her ears, she stabbed the dagger into the Dathgol's eyes, extinguishing the orange glow. Still the squeal crashed through the air with its dangerous cacophony.

With a cry, Armalina stabbed up into the Dathgol's open mouth, ending the monster's shrieks as it slumped to the grass. Echoing silence replaced the discordant noise, until Armalina became aware of her panting breaths. She looked down at the dismembered body on the ground. A throbbing pain began to pulse in her arm and, as she looked down, she saw blood oozing from gashes in her skin.

The Dathgol's teeth had got her, its last action before it died.

Armalina felt a lightness in her head, her body heavy. The pain began to spread towards her shoulder. She collapsed, her eyes looking at her defeated enemy.

All alone again. And dying. She was sure of it. Death would bring a bittersweet absence of pain.

Overwhelmed by tiredness and intensifying pain, she just wanted sleep. If she never woke again, she didn't care. She had lost everything. What else did she have to live for, but for revenge?

Against dragons, what hope did she have? She snorted once, the laugh stealing energy she needed.

Suddenly, she heard the patter of many footsteps and, as she saw what was approaching, she felt fear once more.

Achlonakai.

Armalina counted at least six of the fearsome beasts. She fought her heavy eyes, urging them to stay open. Her brain could barely keep track of events, working extra hard to hear what was happening and understand the data. Her hands rested weakly on the hilt of her dagger.

"She's been bitten," a gruff voice declared. "Prepare the healing herbs."

Armalina tried to speak but her lips felt numb and clumsy.

"Don't strain, girl. You've been mortally wounded." The coarse voice was talking once more. "This poultice should help heal your wounds, but there can be no guarantees. The bite of the Dathgol is poison to all creatures. This might sting some."

Armalina felt the pulsing pain in her arm begin to sting as the Achlonakel rubbed the paste into her wound. The stinging sensation coursed through her body until blackness consumed her senses.

ARMALINA WOKE GRADUALLY, the clearing around her lit by morning's dull grey light. The pain in her arm had devolved into a dull throb. She flexed her elbow, testing it, feeling much better. The Dathgol's body had been removed and, as she looked towards the fire, Armalina saw the Achlonakai whispering and eating long shanks of meat.

She was surprised to find them different to how they had been described. In the cold light of day, she could see they had a pair of human-like arms on a hairy human torso, with a human head. They stood on four tiger paws, making them a strange six-limbed creature. They wiped away the juices dripping down their bearded chins with their hands. Long hair framed rectangular skulls. Their tails swished softly behind them, relaxed and sleepy.

As she watched, she noticed two Achlonakai prowling the perimeter of the clearing, their tails held rigidly in the air as they walked. Each sentry held a sword and shield, like the knights in her father's stories. Occasionally they would sniff the air and pause, triangular ears pointing upwards, before continuing on.

Armalina tried sitting up. Her head was dizzy and she felt woozy, falling back into the soft grass.

"The girl warrior awakens," one of the Achlonakai growled. The pack turned, their pointed faces peering inquisitively as she tried sitting up once more. Some of the group had bows and arrows, while others had sheathed swords strapped around their bodies.

"Good morning, girl. I must say I've seen prettier than you, but considering the circumstances..." The largest Achlonakel, who Armalina assumed was their leader, guffawed at his own joke.

"When your quest is to seek revenge, then beauty is of no issue," Armalina said, her voice sounding braver than she felt. They had saved her life, but she didn't know her position with these beasts yet. Her lack of chains was a positive sign, even considering her weakness and number of opponents.

"And with whom do you seek for revenge, pray tell?" the leader said, stalking closer to her. She had managed to sit up and was now trying to stand while she kept her gaze on the approaching Achlon-akel. Her head swayed, her legs threatening to collapse beneath her.

"Any being who had a part in killing my family. And anyone who stands in my way will fall before me," she said through gritted teeth. Her short black hair was matted to her head, steely blue eyes challenging, determined.

"Are we part of that list?" the leader asked, looking around at his peers, arms stretched out wide. A sneer contorted his face, revealing sharp teeth.

"Only if you're friendly with dragons, or the Dathgol. Or try to stop me leaving," Armalina said.

"We saw you kill the Dathgol. That was very courageous of you. Of course, we would have joined in to help but..." He looked around guiltily at his herd. "Anyway, I am Brutellus. I am the leader of our clan." He held out his human hand to shake. Armalina saw thick, coarse hairs covering the back.

"Armalina." She had no reason to lie about her name.

"Well, Armalina. Come enjoy some roast mutton with us. You must be famished."

Her stomach rumbled, clenching together in rolling waves. "Yes, thank you." She moved over to the fire to join the others.

"Each of us has many roles within our clan. I am our leader. I am responsible for our safety as we migrate through the lands. Whatever we do, we have no alliances outside our clan." Brutellus passed Armalina a shank of meat.

"The Dathgol and the dragons provide many dangers to us. Anybody who can defeat them is our ally. Unless they go against us."

Armalina bit into the tender flesh, feeling the juice dribble down her chin. She wiped it away with her hand, before hungrily licking the smear.

"Only problem is," she said when she had swallowed the morsel, "I have no idea where I am, or where to go. I've no idea where to find the dragons."

Brutellus watched, his eyes inquisitive. "So what's your plan, girl? Just wander around and hope you stumble upon them?" Brutellus sneered as his herd sniggered sycophantically. "Those dragons fell to the world in flames, and now they're going to burn us all. We will be nothing but ashes. What makes you think you will do any better than all the soldiers we watched die in battle yesterday?" Scorn dripped from his words.

Armalina fought back tears, her eyes burning as she stared into the flames. What did she have that could destroy dragons?

"A burning desire for revenge. My dagger. Some spells. A willingness to die in battle, if it comes to it." Her words came out steady and firm.

"Such a massive arsenal," one of the Achlonakai said.

Armalina turned and glared at the speaker. "My father once said that the world needed the small players in a game. While the strong are distracted by their peers, it is those they perceive as weak who sneak through in stealth and light the fires that topple the very foundations they fought to build." She felt herself getting breathless as she recited her father's words. "I'm small enough to sneak into the cracks. Once there I can grow like a weed and break apart stone. I'm not stopping until I have destroyed my target, or died trying."

She stood up, dropped the shank of mutton onto the ground and pulled out her dagger. "Come let me prove it to you," she said to the Achlonakel. "What's your name?"

"It's okay, Armalina. Zcharielus meant no offence," Brutellus said, holding up his palm, placating and calm.

"Well, Zcharielus." She stared into his black eyes. "Starum bladius." She watched as the Achlonakel stood, unmoving, his eyes wavering in fear as if looking for an escape. She walked up to him, circling him as she spoke. "There you stand, under my command. I could have killed you by now, if I desired it. But I won't. As your leader said, you have a very specific role which I am sure is irreplaceable. My father's honour declares I owe you my life for healing my wound, however, don't be naive to think I won't defend myself." Moving away, she relaxed her mind, releasing him from the trance. Her shoulders slumped as she breathed out deeply.

Zcharielus pulled out his sword and stalked towards her, stiletto teeth bared. Life coursed through her body, ready to use her weapon or cast another spell.

"Leave it, Zcharielus!" Brutellus warned. "Very nice trick, Armalina." His voice softened. "We would like to help you before you leave us. Can you read a map?"

She shook her head, embarrassed. "Never seen one," Armalina admitted.

"Thought so. It's surprisingly common outside of castles. Cidrellus, bring a map please."

The Achlonakel grabbed some parchment from a satchel on its back. "Cidrellus is our cartographer and navigator. Amazing sense of direction," Brutellus said as Cidrellus approached.

"Thank you, Cidrellus. Please stay and help our new friend read a map."

Cidrellus smiled, unable to hold her gaze. He kept his eyes focused on the map as he pointed out the landmarks around them, explaining how to gauge direction.

Armalina picked up the meat she had been gnawing on and ate hungrily as she listened, trying not to let the juices smear her chin.

"Do you understand all that?" Cidrellus asked as she threw the bone into the fire.

She nodded, swallowing the meat in her mouth. Her tongue fiddled with some strands of meat stuck between her teeth.

"Reading a map seems incredibly easy," she admitted.

Cidrellus smiled. "Yes, but not for some of us." He looked pointedly at some of his clan. "This map is yours to keep." He rolled it up, shoved it inside a metal ring, and held it out to her. It was only slightly wider than her hand, sticking out either end of her fist.

Brutellus held a leather satchel towards her. "The Dathgol had haunted these grounds for a long time, making it unsafe for us in these parts. Please take these gifts as a token of our appreciation. It may not be much, but it should help you on your journey to defeat the dragons."

Armalina looked inside and saw food, a travelling cloak and some healing herbs.

"Thank you, Brutellus, to you and your clan. I promise not to stop until the dragons have been destroyed. I must say, you're nothing like what I expected."

Brutellus grinned. "Nothing ever is. You can have that advice for free. We have lived a nomadic lifestyle for many years, and our wisdom has been passed down through generations. The biggest lesson I can pass on is this: Things will never be as they appear. Always look beyond the surface if you wish to find the truth. We must leave. We wish you well," Brutellus said, placing his hand on her shoulder.

"Remember, walk that way for what's left of today, and you should reach the kingdom of Emilica. That is where we saw the dragons battling," Cidrellus said. "Remember to watch for landmarks so you don't get lost."

"Thank you, Cidrellus. I hope we can meet after this is all over," Armalina said, slinging the satchel over her shoulder. She turned to walk away.

"Wait up," a croaky voice called out. She turned around and was surprised to see Zcharielus pounding quickly towards her. Placing a hand on her dagger hilt, she prepared to defend herself. Zcharielus slowed his pace and laughed. "I mean you no harm. I have a spare sword and shield, and would like to gift them to you for... for teaching me a few things about duelling."

"These gifts are too much," Armalina mumbled.

"Please take them," Zcharielus said. "These weapons will be more effective than your dagger." He glanced at the weapon at her hip.

"It is more powerful than you think then," she spat defensively. The smile on the Achlonakel's face inflamed her fury.

"You misunderstand me," Zcharielus began. "I agree daggers have their place in battle, especially when there's a need to remain stealthy. But when you see the size of the dragons, you may see my meaning. You will need something bigger. Before we left, we saw a boy who rode a dragon into battle. Perhaps he might be able to help you on your quest, though maybe he might try to stop you. I have faith that you will know what to do." Zcharielus looked at his departing herd. "Goodbye, Armalina." Zcharielus turned and ran off, leaving Armalina standing in the quiet glade, a small wind blowing the hair across her face.

Armalina walked in the direction Cidrellus had pointed, her scalp itchy in the hot sun.

Finally, as the sun was beginning to drop behind the mountains on the horizon, Armalina came to the edge of the forest. She could see scorched land before a towering stone castle.

Flying high in the darkening sky was a dragon, larger than she could have imagined. Riding on its back was the hunched silhouette of a young man.

Armalina had a lot of work ahead of her. After readjusting her satchel, she set off, burning with desire to avenge her family.

She was going to set the world on fire.

Some Other Body

J onathan heard the machines beeping softly, as if his ears were attached to some other body in the distance. His eyes were heavy as he struggled to pry them open. The ceiling above was white, with only a sprinkler and white dome smoke detector—flashing two red dots—to break up the expanse of plainness. Beneath him, the bed was hard and uncomfortable. A feeling of lightness overwhelmed him, making him dizzy and nauseous. He sat up feeling resistance from the cords attached to his skin.

Jonathan fell back down, his head hitting the pillow, where he blacked out.

When he woke some time later, he felt less dizzy and lay, taking in the room around him. Footsteps and muttered conversations echoed in through the open door. He sat up and looked about him at the machines that decorated the room. A monitor showed a rainbow of coloured lines and numbers, though he wasn't sure exactly what they meant. As he stood on the cold linoleum floor, his bare feet felt a strange adhesion, like a thin spread of glue. Jonathan felt as if he was weightless, his legs feeling nothing. The wall held a number of electrical sockets and air valves for oxygen.

In the corner of the room was a chair stacked with bundles of blankets and sheets. His eyes glossed over the room, seeing everything, but not quite taking it in. A water jug sat next to a clear plastic cup on a portable table. Jonathan's mouth felt parched. Moving to the table, he reached out to pick up the cup.

His hand stopped at the plastic. It was like he had no strength.

"What the Hell?" Jonathan said as he tried again to pick up the cup, once more unsuccessfully.

The pile of blankets in the corner moved and made a noise. When he looked more closely, he saw two jeans-covered legs poking out. Whoever it was had kicked off their white sneakers revealing their plain white socks. After he had moved across to the chair, Jonathan tried to move the blankets, but his hand stopped as it had on the cup.

"What is happening?" he said to himself. "Am I a ghost?"

An overwhelming urge to vomit spread through his gut. When he turned back to the bed he saw his body still lying—eyes closed—under the sheets, cords and drains attached in a tangled web. *How am I looking at myself still in bed?* His face was bruised and had certainly looked better before whatever had happened to put him in hospital.

Am I a ghost? he wondered. *Does that mean I'm dead?*

Peering closely at his body in the bed he saw a thick blue tube attached to his nose, like the CPAP breathing apparatus his grandma used. His chest was rising and falling in intermittent patterns beneath the sheets. His body was alive, but did that life extend to his mind?

A scream echoed down the hall and through the door. Chills ricocheted through his spine. Was it a patient, or a family member? Either way, it didn't bode well.

He needed to get out of the room. Walking tentatively to the door, Jonathan peeked out at the busy hallway. Nurses walked carrying clipboards. Visitors sat in chairs sipping hot drinks from Styrofoam cups while they scrolled on their phones. Jonathan walked unnoticed past the people in the hall, unable to focus on any one conversation among the hubbub of noise. Not one pair of eyes seemed to focus on him, instead passing over him in a cursory glance.

As a kid he had always wanted to be invisible. Mainly so he could sneak around unnoticed and be the proverbial fly on the wall. Even though he doubted the practicality of invisibility, especially the genital shrinkage from wearing no clothes in the middle of winter, he never dreamed it would become real. Now he had a chance to explore the hospital, and to see people when they thought they were alone.

Jonathan began to walk away from his room, trying to focus on anything interesting. He strode to a group of doctors who were moving from room to room, a tall trolley holding a computer as someone—a doctor presumably—typed notes. Jonathan felt dumb. They spoke in a medical discourse, their use of jargon hard for him to understand.

Disappointed, he moved on to a woman who was having a hushed conversation in the corner with a man. He moved up to the woman and crouched down, his face right in front of hers. Their noses touched. The woman's eyes peered right through him; it made Jonathan feel like a window.

"But he was caught with the neighbour and his heart stopped. Doctors are saying he may not make it through the night," the woman said. Jonathan felt the wind of her words blow across his face, but when he tried to touch her, his skin met an impenetrable force that wouldn't budge.

"So are we telling Mum, or not?" the man whispered back. Jonathan turned and looked into the man's grey eyes.

"You know we can't tell Mum. It'd break her heart!" the woman said, her blue eyes glassy, rimmed in red.

Jonathan left the siblings to their family issues and moved through the ward. In the worst moments of their life, people were pretty boring. What he really wanted to do was see a surgery taking place, or somebody doing something embarrassing; something to make him laugh. He wandered the halls, peering through open doors and listening out for juicy gossip. By the time he had reached the bank of lifts, he had neither seen nor heard anything of interest. Instinct kicked in, making him attempt to avoid running into people as he walked.

An empty lift was about to close its doors and Jonathan raced forward, his arm outstretched out of habit, forgetting about his lack of physical substance. The lift's doors began to close on him as he slid inside and tried to push a button.

Realisation struck, making him punch the metal wall. How would he make the lift move if he couldn't put pressure on the buttons? Now he was stuck inside the stuffy lift. A pungent stench of stale fart, body odour and cigarette smoke lingered inside the lift, making Jonathan feel queasy. There was nothing he could do but wait and hope somebody would come soon to use the lift.

A sudden thought occurred to him: how would he get back? He would need to rely on somebody getting in who wanted to get to the floor his body was on. Was it even important for him to stay close to his body? If he was a ghost, it meant he was essentially dead. Unless he was, by some miracle, able to relocate his presence back into his body, he would be stuck haunting the world forever. Not that he could really do much in the way of making his presence known, so it would be more like lurking.

Finally the doors opened and a man walked in, a backpack slung over his shoulder, pushing Jonathan back. Jonathan's feet slid on the floor below him, like an avatar in a computer game.

"Hey!" Jonathan called out. The man pushed the button for the ground floor and stood facing away from his invisible companion. Jonathan debated whether he should get out and stay with his body in the room, or stay and walk around a bit. His decision was made for him as the doors closed and Jonathan felt the lift begin to shake as it descended.

The man began picking his nose and, holding his finger in front of him, examined the snot. He rolled it between his finger and thumb before flicking it, where it stuck to the lift wall near the button panel. Jonathan cringed in disgust. His older brother had often left his snot balls on the toilet wall, grossing out the whole family until he had moved out after high school. But, as far as Jonathan knew, Callum had never left them in public like the man in the lift.

When the lift arrived at the ground floor, Jonathan rushed to get away from the snot-flicking man. He would worry about getting back to his body later. For now, he decided, he would explore some more and see what he was capable of. A crowd of people milled around in the ground level foyer. Some were seated in lounges, chatting in groups; others waited in line for coffee at the café gift shop. Jonathan stood, deciding where to go next among the myriad of hallways and doors.

An overwhelming feeling of being watched made his skin tingle, shivers shaking through his body. He looked around, about to ignore his instinct when he saw a woman leaning against the wall, her eyes focussed intently on him. She reminded Jonathan of a young Elton John, her blonde hair cut short, fringe dangling down to round, sparkly glasses. Her dress was adorned in sequins that refracted colourful specks of light across the floor, like a rainbow mirror ball. When she saw Jonathan returning her gaze, she smiled, yellow teeth peeking from beneath dry, cracked lips.

Jonathan felt his eyebrows crease together as he peered behind him at the beige wall. He moved towards the window to his left, peering out at the busy street of the city outside where people moved about. All part of their normal life, unaware of the number of lives that change each day inside the hospital near them. Peering back at the woman, Jonathan saw she had begun to move towards him, a smile lighting up her face.

How can she see me? Jonathan wondered, dreading conversation. He had never been great around new people. Small talk had never been his forte.

"Another planer," the woman said cheerily. Her voice seemed too loud for a hospital foyer, easily heard over the quiet hubbub. "Hi. It's been ages since I met someone like me." She held her hand out towards him. Stunned, Jonathan took it in his hand and they shook.

"You *can* speak, can't you? Your tongue ain't cut out or nothin'? I met a dude a year or two back who was deaf. Can't 'member what happened to him. Think he was pushed onto the road or somethin' and ended up bein' taken along on the front of a truck. Least that's what Karen said after, but. Never did trust her, if you get me. Anyway, listen to me rabbit on. Just I haven't had anyone to talk to in…" the woman paused, her right hand scratching her head. "Just under a year? Hard to keep track of time here, what with every day bein' same as the last. Also, get used to no sleep. Some reason us planers can get no sleep. You *are* a planer, ain't ya?" The woman's head tilted to the side as if weighing up whether Jonathan had enough brains to respond.

"What do you mean?" Jonathan asked, looking around at the people around them, all oblivious to their presence. "What's a... a planer?"

"Taylor told me about it when I first found myself like this." She swept her hand down her body and stopped talking, looking around her.

"What do you mean? Like, dressed or something?" Jonathan asked, squinting in confusion.

"Huh?" The woman looked at him. "What's your name, bud?"

"Jonathan. Yours?"

"Marianna. Anyway, so, are you?" She began looking impatient.

"Am I what? A planer thingy?" Jonathan asked. This was why he hated talking to new people.

"Yeah. We were only just, like, talkin' about it. Are you special or somethin'?" Her tone reminded Jonathan of the cliquey girls in his high school, who seemed to irritate anyone who wasn't part of their group.

"Yeah, well it'd help if you kinda explained what they are!" Overwhelmed with frustration, Jonathan was thinking about leaving and hoping he would find another *planer*. He breathed deeply before exhaling.

"A planer is someone who has left their body while they're in a coma," Marianna explained as if to a toddler. "They're like us, and can move around freely, but can't move any objects or talk to living people. A strong fart'd prob'ly move us."

"So, we're ghosts?"

"No, we ain't dead! It's called astral protection, or something."

Jonathan sniggered. "You mean astral projection." He stopped laughing when he saw Marianna's glare. "Sorry... But why are we called planers?"

Her glare remained on her face like a grotesque mask. "Because we're on the astral *plane*. Duh!"

"So if you're a planer, you're still in a coma?" Jonathan asked. "Is your body in this hospital? What happened to you?" He had lots of questions to ask, and had to hold them from bursting out at once.

"That's a bit personal." Marianna put her hands on her hips. "Why don't you tell me what happened to *you*?"

"Well, that's the thing. I don't really remember. My body's upstairs on Level Ten, though." Jonathan glanced up at the ceiling in the direction he thought his body lay in bed.

"How do ya not remember what happened? I remember ev'ry detail of mine. Ev'ry punch and kick; my partner screamin' at me till I blacked out. My body's kept alive by a machine. I heard my mum call me a vegetable, but she's too chicken shit to turn off the life support. Thinks I'll wake up or somethin'." Her lips puckered and twisted to the side like she had swallowed something sour. "I tell ya, I just wanted to strangle her, just so she knew how close I was standin'. Anyway, I've been waitin' for my body to be better. I kinda want to be alive again."

"What happens if our bodies die?" Jonathan asked, looking around them, a weird feeling igniting in his gut.

"I dunno for sure. Say, how's your body? Did it look okay?" Marianna asked, gazing intently into his eyes.

"Umm. I guess it was okay. I mean, it was alive and not too badly injured. From what I could see anyway."

Marianna glanced towards the lifts. Jonathan followed her gaze and saw a group of people waiting to go up, one woman holding a teddy bear.

"I'm gonna go see it. You can wait here if you like," Marianna said, beginning to walk quickly towards the lifts.

"Hey, no! I don't want you to!" Jonathan called, suddenly worried.

"Too bad. I'm just gonna have a little go in it anyway. I heard that I can have a go in your body and wanna try it out. You won't even miss it."

"No, it's mine!" Jealousy burned within him. Jonathan grabbed her shoulder, trying to force her back. She spun around and punched him in the nose. Pain exploded in his head as he fell backwards. White light clouded his vision as he tried to stand back up. Instinctively he felt for blood, before remembering he was not in his body anymore.

Slowly, his vision cleared and he saw Marianna going in to the lifts, riding on a man's back. Her arms were thrown around his neck, her feet around his hips, like he had seen toddlers and koalas do.

The centre lift's doors began to close and Marianna, who was now facing Jonathan, grinned devilishly.

"No!" Jonathan called, racing forward, his arm outstretched. He slammed into the lift doors painlessly, sagging to the ground. He felt embarrassed sobbing in public, until he remembered nobody could see him. Nobody could hear him.

Nobody could help him.

And the only other person who knew he existed was currently in the lift, on her way to take his body from him. And with Jonathan in his incorporeal form, there would be nothing he could do to stop her.

He needed to get back to his body. Nervous and impatient, Jonathan waited for the lift doors to open again. With all his thought, he tried to push the call buttons, but his luck didn't change.

"Come on. Go up, somebody!" he called into the foyer.

Finally, after a few minutes, a man walked up to the lifts and pushed the button. He was wearing a backpack, leaving no room for Jonathan to copy Marianna and jump on his back.

When the lift door opened, Jonathan rushed in, hoping the man pushed the button to his own level. He was in the lift to the left of the centre one. Had Marianna been able to get to the tenth level where his body lay defenceless? Or was she stuck in limbo, moving to other levels?

The man in the lift pushed the button for Level Eight.

"Shit!" Jonathan said, wishing he had his body back. It had been so easy to do things with his body.

The man rushed off when the lift arrived, leaving Jonathan anxious with indecision. If he got off the lift, he would then have to wait for someone else to get on a different lift, and hope he made it up to his own floor. On the other hand, if he waited in this lift, he might be waiting for hours before somebody else got back on. Then he would have to wait for the lift to go to his floor. Meanwhile, he could be missing a lift to Level Ten.

Jonathan decided it would be safer to stay on this lift, and hope it took him to Level Ten before Marianna. As much as he hated a lot of his life, he couldn't let her steal it from him. Sure, there was a lot he wished he could change, and he was glad to give those up to somebody else.

But the happy moments. Those were what he lived for. He could not let her steal those away.

Pushing random buttons while he waited, Jonathan planned what he would do if he ever made it to Level Ten.

His stomach jolted as he felt the floor vibrate beneath him, shuddering its way downwards.

Wrong way, he thought. When the lift had reached the foyer, its doors opened, a wave of people pushing their way inside. A flurry of fingers pushed buttons and, with a gleam of hope, Jonathan saw the large '10' illuminated in blue.

"Finally!" he said, feeling energised. He felt his hand tapping his thigh as he waited for the lift to stop at each level.

"Hold the doors, please!" a doctor called when they had stopped at Level Six. She continued talking to a nurse, as if it was an important, but rushed conversation.

"Come on, come on," Jonathan muttered, wishing he could close the doors. The doctor scribbled something on a clipboard before rushing into the lift.

"Sorry. Thanks for waiting," the doctor said as she moved to the back of the lift. The doctor pressed the button for Level Ten absentmindedly, checking her phone as they rose. A recorded message announced Level Ten and the doctor rushed out, Jonathan on her heels. He rushed to his room, overtaking the doctor when she spoke to another nurse. Jonathan hoped Marianna was still stuck in the lift.

Even if she wasn't in his room, he had no idea how to reconnect with his body. He didn't even know how he had disconnected with it in the first place. Perhaps she had been lying and he really was a ghost. She might be hiding in a corner, laughing at his pointless rush to get back to his body. A quick glance around him as he ran revealed no sign of Marianna.

Inside the room, Jonathan's body lay on the bed, unmoving. The consistent beep of the monitor showed he was still alive. At a glance the room seemed just as he had left it.

Then he saw her.

How he had missed her, Jonathan wasn't sure. Marianna was sitting on his chest, facing away from the door. She was staring out at a helicopter that was coming in to land on the roof, bringing a patient for urgent care. She snapped out of her trance, and began to turn in the bed, lifting her legs onto his own.

Silently, hoping to keep his advantage of surprise, Jonathan ran to her. She heard his footsteps as they pounded the floor, their echoes going unheard in the physical world. He leapt over the bed, his arms out to tackle her, like he had learnt playing footy in his youth. They tumbled to the floor, entwined in a tight embrace. Teeth bared, Marianna screamed out as she fought furiously to escape Jonathan's clutches. She bit his neck, pain flaring across his shoulders as he howled.

Jonathan began punching her head, dull thumps echoing from her skull. A tsunami of pain flared in his groin as her knee slammed into his nuts, his hands moving to protect them from another hit.

Marianna stood up, kicking him as he curled in agony, leaping once more onto the bed. Ignoring the pain, Jonathan got to his knees and reached up to Marianna, who was sitting on his body again. She tried to hold herself in place, but was unsuccessful as she was pulled down, falling next to Jonathan. Her head hit the ground with a soft crack and Jonathan, who moved slowly with pain, placed his shin across her neck. Her mouth was contorted in a grimace as she grunted beneath him.

"Stay away from my body," he panted. Jonathan could feel her legs flailing behind him as she tried to kick him while struggling to breathe. He punched her mouth, feeling the adrenaline surge through him in the fight for his life.

When he felt his adversary go limp beneath him, he stopped, watching her mouth agape, shallow breaths forcing their way between her lips. Jonathan stood up gingerly, staring down at the woman on the floor. The woman who tried to steal his body almost looked peaceful, as if she couldn't do anything as terrible as stealing someone else's body.

The door opened, making Jonathan turn defensively, ready to fight once more. The doctor from the lift walked in, reading Jonathan's chart. A stethoscope was draped around her neck, bouncing on her white coat as she wrote down the numbers from the monitor. She moved to his body and listened to his chest with her stethoscope, frowning in concentration.

In the corner of the room, the bundle of sheets began to move, and a familiar head emerged from beneath.

"You must be Mrs Forbes," the doctor said, looking over at Jonathan's mother. "I'm Doctor Libby. I'm Jonathan's doctor. How are you holding up? That chair mustn't be very comfortable."

Jonathan's mother gave a weak smile. "No, but I don't think I'd be getting any more sleep in a comfortable bed, considering the circumstances. I still can't... It's just..."

Jonathan moved across to her and threw his arms around her, wanting to feel her warmth. Wanting her to feel his presence. Her tears overwhelmed him with guilt, and he struggled to hold back his own.

"Mum, I'm here," he said, holding her shoulders and staring into her glassy eyes. "I'm here. Please feel me. I'm here."

Her eyes looked right through him at the doctor, who moved towards his mum and placed a hand on her shoulder. "We think he will pull through. This coma is to help repair his brain. He's recovered a lot since he came to us. His brain was starved of oxygen, so we won't know the full extent of damage until he wakes up. Do you have any questions?"

"Lots. Not much you can answer at the moment, I suppose," Mrs Forbes said between sobbing breaths. "I have lots of questions for Johnny, if..." She paused. "When he wakes up." She moved over and took Jonathan's hand in hers.

He closed his eyes and tried to imagine he could feel it. What had happened to him? How did he wind up here?

"Will he have any lasting damage or anything?" Mrs Forbes asked, staring at her son's comatose body.

"It's hard to be sure until he wakes up. The scans yesterday didn't show too much damage to his brain, but with brains it's difficult to judge full function until we see him awake. I'm sorry, Mrs Forbes, but we need to let him recover and let his body repair itself." Doctor Libby glanced down at her patient. "He's in good hands here."

Mrs Forbes answered with silence.

"Please buzz if you need anything. I'll be back in a few hours to check on you both. Would you like me to organise a social worker to come see you?"

Jonathan's mum nodded, still staring tearfully at her son. "Please," she mumbled.

"I'll do that now. Please try to get some rest. If you do go home, we can call you if anything changes."

"I'll just stay here, I think." Doctor Libby placed her hand once more on Mrs Forbes' shoulder, before leaving quietly.

"Why, Jonathan?" his mum asked. "Why did you do it?"

"I didn't... I don't know," Jonathan said, forgetting she couldn't hear him.

"When I saw you in the bathtub, I thought you had... I thought you were... dead. You said you were okay after that *thing* with Mark. I knew you were drinking every night, but I thought it was a phase.

I thought you were okay… Please, wake up, Jonathan." His mum whimpered. "Please."

Jonathan kissed her forehead. "I'm gonna try, Mum. I'm gonna try." He clambered on to the bed, glancing furtively at Marianna on the floor. The pain from his struggle had subsided to a dull throb. Kneeling on his own chest was the weirdest feeling he had ever had, looking searchingly in his own face for answers. How did he reconnect with his body?

He tried shoving his hand in his mouth—fingers first—and seeing how far he got, but his lips remained partially closed, stubborn and unmoving. Next he copied what he had seen Marianna doing and sat on his chest, thinking how wonderful it would be to wake in his body, once more a corporeal being.

Still nothing happened.

Maybe I need to lay down on my body, like a toddler's puzzle, he thought.

Just as he was about to wriggle down to lay on his own body, a sweeping force threw him from the bed to the floor, where he slid to the door. His head cracked against the immoveable wood, leaving him dazed, his vision blurry.

Looking up at where he had been only seconds ago, he saw Marianna smirking down at him as she climbed onto his chest.

"Thanks for the body, Johnny Boy. Your mum's gonna *love* me!" Marianna said, giving him a quick wave as she slid down to lay on his body, moving beneath his mum's drooped head above his torso. Jonathan fought through the haziness to stand up and rush to the bed.

As suddenly as she had appeared, Marianna had disappeared. He looked down at the ground, expecting her to have slid off, but she was nowhere in sight. The monitors beside him began to beep more quickly, his vital signs improving.

"No, no, no," he said, feeling his heart beat faster. His hands were sweaty as he clawed at his body, trying to find some way to drag Marianna out, desperate for his body back. "No! You bitch!"

A roar of anguish escaped his mouth, hurting his throat. "That's *my* body!"

The eyelids on his face began to flicker, and he felt his body twitch beneath him.

Beside the bed, his mum began stirring, her face filled with hope as she looked up at the monitors, then at her son's body.

"Jonathan! You're awake!" Mrs Forbes cried, before pushing the button to call the nurse.

"Hi... *Mum*," Jonathan—the fake one—mumbled through cracked lips, looking around the room, before focussing on the woman in front of him.

"My baby boy." Mrs Forbes leaned forward to hold her son in a teary embrace. An embrace full of warmth that Jonathan should have been feeling. Instead, a feeling of cold dread washed over him as he climbed to the floor, shoulders slumped.

"I'm your baby boy," Jonathan muttered. He stood watching the exchange, despair drilling into his gut. With each passing moment, the pain seemed to grow inside him until he could bear it no longer.

As he began walking out of the room, a nurse came briskly in, ignoring the soul of her patient as she passed. Jonathan stood at the threshold, looking out at the ward. Lonely among a sea of people.

He began walking aimlessly down the hallway, peering in to each room, looking for another soul or a comatose body. Or some way to get his own body back. Some way to be back with his family. He knew he would be lonely until he found someone like him.

Until he could inhabit some other body.

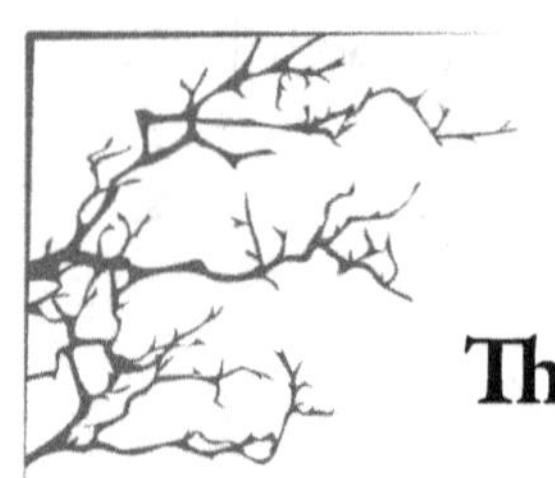

Through the Fog

The mist swept onto the beach, driving away the hot sunshine. Cool droplets washed over Katie's skin, forming goose bumps. She stood up, leaving her son to build his sandcastle. A shiver vibrated down her spine as she watched the waves wash onto the sand. Tendrils of fog danced on the water's surface.

"Come on, Lincoln. Let's go to the car," Katie said, bending to collect the toys. She winced as Lincoln began to squeal, tears forming in his eyes.

Snot had begun to bubble in his nostrils, a total meltdown building within him.

"I know you're upset about leaving, darling, but we need to go. This fog is scaring me! I want to go find the car and go home. We'll stop and get a burger and chips on the way home, how about that?" Lincoln nodded. Katie peered through the mist towards the sea. Earlier, she had seen the horizon, the light blue of the sky darkening as it moved down behind them.

Now, she saw only a blanket of mist, shades of grey embracing them on the sand. She reached down to pick up her bawling son, who thrashed in her arms.

"My shovel!" he squealed into her ear. "Bucket!"

"Okay, darling. You're okay. I'll get your toys," Katie said. As she squatted down to pick up the sand-covered toys, a dark shadow caught her eye. She paused, squinting into the fog. The silhouette of a tall ship emerged through the misty curtain.

It must be some kind of pleasure cruise, Katie thought. *Off-course or searching for land and unable to see?* With Lincoln jerking in her arms, struggling to escape her clutches, Katie waited, watching the ship. She had only ever seen ships like these in movies and photos. The novelty of its appearance piqued her interest.

"Mummy! Mummy! What's that?" Lincoln asked, stopping his struggles to watch the intruder to their secluded beach. Katie put him down, where he wrapped his arm around her leg, his head resting against her thigh.

"It's a ship, darling. Like in your pirate stories."

"Are there pirates, too?" he asked, his embrace tightening.

"I don't know," Katie said, too quickly. "No, it won't be pirates." She didn't want him scared. He'd be even more difficult to manage then. Clingier. Whinier.

The ship moved slowly, edging through the water, its sails looking ripped and torn. It didn't look like it was stopping. *No way could this ship be a pleasure cruise.*

"Let's move back a bit, hey?" Katie said. She began moving back, her son still clamped to her leg, his feet dragging in the sand. Their movements were tracked in the beach, scattered among the demolished sandcastles.

"One. Two. Three. Four." Lincoln was pointing at the ship.

"What're you counting there, munchkin?" Katie asked, peering through the haze.

"Ten! There's ten sticks coming out of the side of its pole, Mummy!" Lincoln declared.

"Mast, darling. It's called a mast."

"Where are all the pirates, Mummy?"

"There aren't any pirates, darling. But I don't know where the people are," Katie admitted. He had a point: *Where was everybody? Had the ship brought the fog with it? Or did the fog bring the ship?*

The ship's keel ran aground, continuing up the beach with a loud scraping sound. As it moved, the wooden planks began to break noisily, splitting, collapsing beneath the weight of the ship. Fog swirled around the slowing movement, and Katie could see the wood had rotted. She was surprised it had lasted so long in the water. The ship leaned forward as it came to a stop, resting on the crumbled ruins of its hull.

"Mummy, I'm scared!" Lincoln declared beside her.

"I know, munchkin. But it's okay. It's just a deserted ship."

"It stinks. I wanna go home!" It did reek. It smelled like her bin a few weeks ago when she hadn't emptied it, and the chicken carcass had begun to decay. That was the morning she didn't need coffee to wake up. The maggots crushing under her feet were enough to freak her out, with more crawling from the bin. She'd been late to work that day, having to vacuum each slimy bug. She'd watched them wriggle in the dust as she emptied the chamber into her wheelie bin, where they had evolved into small, dark flies.

Is it just rotting wood, or is there something else aboard? Katie wondered as she began walking after Lincoln, who had started moving away.

But something drew her back. Something was emerging from the foggy wreck. *Is that an arm?*

She stopped. She felt as if she was being dragged toward the wreck, like an invisible rope was wrapped around her. As she got closer, more limbs began to emerge from the mist, dangling lifelessly through the cracks in the hull. The skin was white and wrinkly, with black bruises blemishing the limbs, scattered among pus-filled lumps. The misty tendrils thickened around her, sending another shiver through her body.

"Lincoln," she called. Her eyes remained focussed on the bodies. Silence echoed around her. "Lincoln!" she called again, desperation etching deep grooves into her voice. When she peered through the milky air, she could see nothing but the mist. She thought she could see dark figures drop from the ship and stumble past her. She backed away and spun around, becoming disoriented in the surrounding mist.

A piercing scream cut through the vapour. She could identify that voice anywhere: her son.

"Lincoln!" she called, spinning around, trying to get her bearings. "Lincoln, where are you?" Fear gripped at her heart, threatening to tear it from the arteries and veins and out through her chest.

"Mummy!" Lincoln squealed. Katie began running in the direction of his voice, stumbling through the thickening mist. "Mummy, the pirates have got me!"

"Shit," she muttered, her head swivelling around, searching for any sign of movement in the swirling fog. Katie began running forwards, unsure if her direction was correct. She didn't want to just stand around and wait for something to happen. Lincoln's voice began to drift away so, turning on her heels, she began running back the way she had come. Or was she? It was hard to tell.

"Mummy!" Lincoln's voice was getting louder again. Quickening her pace, Katie felt her feet struggling in the sand, her legs burning with exertion. The hulking silhouette of the ship began to fill the mist in front of her, and as she approached it, she began to see a hustle of movement. Her feet began splashing in cold water and she slowed her pace, looking up. Lincoln was looking over the edge of the ship, screaming for her help.

But she had no way to get to him quickly.

A sinking feeling overwhelmed her gut. She had failed as a parent.

A new determination steeled her muscles and she began wading through the water towards the slowly departing ship. If she moved fast enough, she could reach it. She could see a web of ropes dangling down, and the rotting wood formed a series of footholds to help her ascend to the deck. As she watched, the ship seemed to repair itself. The rotted wood replaced piece by piece with fresh timber. Holes in the hull were filling with wooden planks.

Katie blinked with confusion, feeling as if her eyes were imagining it all.

Ignoring the chill of the water, icy against her hot skin, she continued pacing through the rippling water. With each step the depth increased, creeping further up her body until she was forced to start swimming. Salty water splashed in her mouth as she tried to keep her head above the surface, watching as the ship swept further from the shore, the mist obscuring her vision. Further from Katie.

Further from safety.

She needed to keep moving, summoning strength and speed to get closer to Lincoln. Her soggy clothes dragged her down, making her feel sluggish and uncoordinated.

Hope drained away; dread swamping her with the cold water soaking her clothes. Her muscles burned—contrasted against the icy water.

The ship's shadow disappeared in the mist ahead, increasing Katie's feeling of hopelessness. Her hair hung wetly on her face, searching in her mouth for warmth, making her taste the saltwater.

Finally the mist began to thin, the sun lighting up the sea in bright glittery sparkles. Katie stopped swimming, searching for the ship. For her son.

It had disappeared. Her son had disappeared.

The horizon was clear, solid light blue over the dark water, broken only by the glowing patches of the sun. She turned around, searching for Lincoln.

Where's the ship? Where's Lincoln? Behind her, the wall of mist rose to infinite heights, swirling tendrils probing the water as far as she could see. Unless the ship had travelled sideways, it had disappeared.

The water felt warmer past the fog, yet Katie still felt cold as she paddled in the water, stagnant. Memories of Lincoln raced through her head, clashing with images of him fighting against kidnappers. Lonely and desperate, she whirled around in the water, searching for any clue of the ship's whereabouts, where it could have gone.

The wall of fog drifted away from her. Or was she drifting away from the fog? She couldn't be sure, but she knew she didn't want to go back into the fog and possibly feel lost forever. The sea extended endlessly on either side. With tiring muscles, Katie decided to continue swimming further to sea, hoping to find some sign of her son or the ship.

If she couldn't find Lincoln, she would die trying.

Katie bobbed on the swells of water, pumping her limbs to propel her away from the fog. The sun began to drop below the haze, shining in her eyes when she turned to check the distance of the mist. If it wasn't for the retreating fog, Katie would have felt like she was making no progress in the water, with no other markers to help her judge the distance.

A sudden thought made her stop. What if the ship had sunk and was now lying on the ocean floor? Surely it couldn't have just disappeared into thin air, or some kind of portal? She had seen no sign of turbulence in the water, no sign of the ship lying deep below the waves.

After looking around her for flotsam in the water, she began dipping her head beneath the surface until she needed air. The water was murky, as if the mist had spread through the sea, down to the sandy depths of the ocean floor. Katie continued searching, diving deeper, moving back towards the fog, hoping to see some clue of the ship beneath the water.

With every dive, Katie felt heavier, struggling more against the pull of the water, like a magnetic force. Salty air filled her nostrils as she breathed heavily, exhausted and desperate, wanting to find some sign of the ship, but seeing nothing. Dusk had fallen as the sun dropped behind the wall of fog, the sky darkening more quickly.

There would be no way she could find Lincoln in the darkness, and the thought stunned her into a numb stillness. She felt the ocean embrace her and let it take her down, eyes closed against the darkness, hoping when she opened them again she would see Lincoln smiling back at her. She held her breath until her chest burned, panicking only slightly when the water flooded her lungs, and the blackness took over her senses.

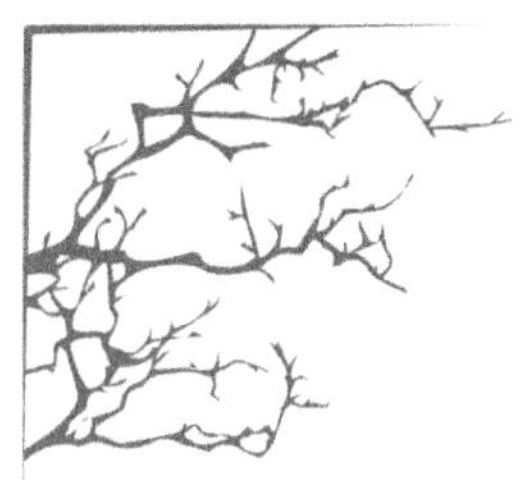

Deserted

Brian would be late to his own funeral. His family and friends had always told him so, and now he would prove them right.

What really made his heart race faster than the car he was driving was that it was his daughter's wedding he would be late for. His only child, getting married. And he would be sneaking in late, trying not to be noticed.

Except everyone *would* notice. He was supposed to be giving Ingrid away to Trent, and hadn't looked forward to the spectacle of walking up the aisle. Brian had planned to be early, but when he was dressed and ready to go, his car surprised him with a flat battery. Of course, he couldn't wear his best suit while changing the battery, so he had changed it wearing only his underwear. Sweat poured down his torso as he connected the battery, and regardless of his experience with cars, it had still taken longer than he had expected. Then, as if he was tainted with bad luck, he needed to change a flat tyre as well, his anger making it hard to concentrate on the task at hand. Ingrid was going to be livid when he rocked up late.

He had promised to be on time. Early even. Unusually early.

Once again, he had broken his promise.

Despite Ingrid's many pleading requests, he was still going to let her down.

He watched the clouds of dust billow behind his speeding car, feeling the tyres slip on the gravel road. High above the horizon, the sun shone, baking the earth below. Brian drove through the swirling shimmers of heat as they rose from the dirt road he knew well. Lines of skinny trees stood sentry on either side of the road, branches out as if feeling for nonexistent rain. Dodging the potholes in the road was almost second nature, but in his rush, they came up more quickly than he remembered.

He was too far out of town for phone reception, so he planned to ring closer to the venue, although he doubted whether anyone would answer if they were on time to begin the ceremony.

The dogleg turn in the road approached, and Brian, glimpsing a dingo in his path, braked on the loose gravel. The car fishtailed, sliding as it tried to fight a lack of friction. He turned the steering wheel, hoping to correct the turn, and felt the car tilt on its side.

There was a moment in time where he knew he had made a massive mistake, and hoped it wouldn't be fatal as time seemed to slow down. Leaning against the tilt, Brian held on to the wheel, foot heavy on the brake. The car began to roll and Brian felt the seatbelt dig into his body as gravity threw him towards the roof. Thunderous noise echoed through the car as the roof slid on the gravel and down the embankment, while a menagerie of wedding presents and rubbish fell to the ceiling. A spider web of fractures spread across the windscreen. The window beside him exploded in a flurry of glass. Brian's hands flew towards the ceiling as he fell, his body cradled painfully in his seatbelt.

Once the car had come to rest on its roof, Brian peered through the cracked windows, looking for the dingo among the dense bushes and straw-like grass. If it had survived, it had not followed him down the declivity.

Brian's body hurt on the right side, like a thousand needles digging in to his skin. His two limbs were the epicentres of pain, and he hoped they weren't fractured, or worse—broken.

With clumsy fingers he unbuckled himself and fell in an awkward heap on the roof, his body collapsing on his bent neck, causing an uproar of pain. Grimacing, Brian moved so he was lying on the roof. He could feel the pebbles of broken glass beneath him, and thought it was worse than the Lego he used to step on in Ingrid's room when she was younger. The mobile phone he kept in the centre crevice lay outside the car, bent and shattered. It would be of no use to him.

He crawled out through the window into the red dirt, dry and dusty as it plumed from his touch. His neck burned in the sun, his white dress shirt sticking to his skin.

Dragging his right limbs, Brian wormed his way to the warm shadows of a nearby tree. It offered a little protection from the summer sun, but it was much better than the blazing midday heat. Pretty soon, the car would feel like an oven, even with the broken windows. As he sat propped against the thin, spiky trunk, he licked his parched lips. He regretted bringing no food or water with him, thinking only of rushing to the wedding. He was lucky to have remembered to pack his suit and tie in the back seat of the car, where they now lay with the rest of the jetsam on the ceiling.

Thinking back, he had been surprised to hear his daughter was getting married, particularly after being stuck between two feuding and spiteful parents. Brian supposed she had as good a chance at making marriage work with Trent as anyone else, perhaps even better. He seemed decent enough. A little timid and feminine, but he seemed to genuinely love Ingrid. It was better than some creep on Tinder.

And no matter what choices Ingrid made, Brian would be there to support her.

Except today, on one of her most important days.

Tears began to fall down his cheeks and he wiped them away, embarrassed. He hadn't cried since he was a boy. Even when his life broke down after divorcing his witch of an ex-wife, his eyes remained dry, his heart hard as rock.

His stone heart was beginning to crumble. The land around him was quiet; the air still. Normally he enjoyed the solitude that encompassed his house; land he had bought to escape his depressing life and reconnect with nature. He never saw anybody unless he chose to make the long trip into town to collect his mail or pick up his groceries.

Nobody usually came to visit, yet a strange part of him liked that. He could see cars approach from a great distance, and knew he'd never have Jehovah's Witnesses or sales people come to annoy him. Brian could finally be himself without fear of judgement, something he could never do in his fifteen years of being married.

Fifteen long, arduous, torturous years.

But, hurt and in need of help, he wished there were more people around. More of some kind of semblance of civilisation.

A rustling noise brought him back to the present. His dry lips were sticking together, his eyes itchy and sore as they searched around him.

A brown snake was slithering towards him, its curving body gliding over sticks and stones. Brian looked around for a stick. He knew the snake was venomous, and one bite would be fatal. He needed it gone!

There was a snakebite kit in his car, but it was no use in his current predicament. There was no time.

Reaching up with his left hand, Brian grabbed a branch and broke it off, straining to hold the weight of his body until the wood snapped. It was dry and brittle with a leafless network of twigs at the end, but it was hopefully enough to fend off the approaching serpent.

Brian stabbed the branch at the snake, pushing it backwards. Momentarily. Still the snake slithered more slowly towards him, only a metre away.

He tried again, this time clubbing the snake, watching as the twigs broke around the snake's advancing body. With each hit, the branch became shorter and shorter, until all that remained was the thicker length of wood. The snake was now only an arm's length away.

In a last ditch effort, Brian used the thick end to stab the snake. With repeated thrusts, Brian slammed the branch down on the snake, until its middle section was a bloody pulp. The snake writhed, only inches away.

With his left arm, Brian wiped away the sweat on his face, the white cotton sleeve soaking it up. Then he used the stick to push the snake's wriggling carcass away, just in case it was still alive and able to bite him.

Brian watched as the blood dried quickly. His thoughts turned to the big bottle of cold water sitting in his fridge at home. The saltiness of the sweat on his lip only increased his thirst.

A howl whistled through the air and, as Brian looked up at the road, he saw the dingo that had caused the accident. It stood at the edge, watching Brian and licking its chops as if it could sense his weakness.

If he stayed under the tree, the dingo would have an easy dinner. Brian's stick would be more useful with a functioning dominant hand. He felt weak and clumsy using his left hand.

Keeping the weight off his right foot, Brian began trying to stand up. He held the branch loosely in his right hand and used his left to help pull him upright. Hopefully his height would make the dingo more wary. Unable to walk, Brian began hopping away from the dingo, away from his car. The trees on either side moved past slowly, sagging in the heat.

The dingo followed, body rigid, keeping a safe distance. Its eyes never left Brian, intent on the kill.

Focussing only on continuing to hop forwards, Brian ignored the dingo. Until it howled once more, sounding closer. Turning on his good foot, Brian held the stick out in front of him, ready to go down fighting. He wasn't sure how much damage he could cause, but maybe enough to scare it off. Maybe he could still make it to the wedding reception, if he could keep moving.

If he could kill the mutt, then he could try it for dinner. It couldn't be any worse than his ex-wife's cooking, he thought. Brian rested his right foot on the ground, applying enough pressure to steady himself, a small wave of pain spreading through his leg.

Still the dingo approached, its pink tongue licking the drool on its jaws. It howled again, creeping forwards.

Using the branch as a sword, Brian jabbed forward, yelling as he did.

Still it continued forward.

Brian took a limping step backwards, swinging the branch back and forth, using it as a shield.

The dingo stopped, sniffing the air. With one last look at Brian, the animal turned and scarpered into the bush on the other side of the road. Brian breathed a sigh of relief, wiping the grimy sweat from his forehead.

Until he saw why the dingo had fled.

In the distance, over to his left, Brian could see his car rolled down the embankment. Small flames burned under the bonnet, sending dark grey smoke billowing upwards. The fire had spread to the dry bracken around it, clawing up towards the towering gum trees in the bush nearby.

"Shit!" Brian muttered through dry lips, unable to look away as the flames jumped up, hanging on to the overhanging branches. Within seconds the fire had engulfed the tree and was climbing over its neighbours, free and unchallenged. The wood crackled as it burned, a wall of dark black smoke rising above.

Throwing the stick down, Brian turned and jogged, ignoring the pain thundering through his limping right leg. He breathed through gritted teeth, his mind repeating every swear word he knew in an effort to divert his attention from the pain. With a glance over his shoulder, Brian saw a tsunami of fire coming towards him. Smouldering panic burned within him. There was no way he could outrun this fiery monster.

He stepped into a pothole, his right foot instinctively trying to stop him falling, bringing only pain. Brian began to tilt forwards, his arms outstretched to protect his body. He tumbled, more pain grazing its way into his skin, his breath knocked out of his lungs.

Watching the smoke darken the sky above, he lay, his body registering the overwhelming pain. His throat burned as he tried to regain his breath.

Slowly, he looked up at the flames towering high above, fuelled by many years of drought and dusty dryness. The fire had raced ahead, and now encircled his prone body, stealing the oxygen from the air around him.

Every breath was a burning struggle, and he felt the energy drain from his muscles, realisation dawning in him.

He wouldn't make it out alive.

As the flames began to engulf him, Brian smiled at the irony. His body would be barely intact and it would take them some time to identify him, charred beyond recognition.

The fire would make him late to his own funeral.

Wish Upon A Star

Dakota and Conor watched the falling star streak across the sky. The waning moon struggled to illuminate the beach below with its dim light. Reaching out his hand, Dakota grabbed Conor's hand, returning her smile. A cool breeze blew across the sand, dancing with the waves crashing in from the dark sea. The star disappeared into the universe beyond the darkness.

"Did you make a wish?" Dakota asked. He looked back out at the smudge of light on the water, painted by the weak moon.

"Yeah, I did," Conor said, her teeth glowing white in the darkness. "But I can't tell you or it won't come true." She giggled and leaned in, kissing him passionately on the lips.

"That's just an old wives' tale. It's not like wishes come true anyway, so how could telling me your wish stop it from happening?" Their noses touched as they looked in each other's eyes. "Do you think there's some kind of wish-granting genie waiting to see if someone will keep their wish to themselves?"

"What if there *is* a spiritual genie? One we can't see? He might just be waiting for one of us to make a wish and keep it a secret so he can grant it." Conor grinned. "Maybe he disappears in a puff of smoke when you share the wish with someone else."

"How long do you have to keep it secret for? Is he going to grant the wish, then hang around in case you let someone else in on your wishy secret? Surely he can't be around forever, presuming he exists, of course."

"Fair point, but maybe genies are like God. He exists, but you never get a chance to see or feel him. You just have to believe," Conor said, grinning impishly and stroking his leg. She rubbed her bare feet against his leg coquettishly. "What if mine *did* come true? You'd like it to come true, trust me."

"I'll tell you mine if you tell me yours," Dakota said, nuzzling into her neck and nibbling softly. He enjoyed the way she shivered when he did that, but pulled away teasingly. "I'll tell you mine anyway. I don't like keeping secrets from you. Genie or no genie."

"No, don't tell me. It's not going to come true otherwise."

"Let me kiss a star on your face while I tell you," Dakota said. "First, I'll kiss your forehead, the top point of your star."

Conor moaned, her eyes closed and lips pouted. "Next, I kiss your two cheeks beneath your beautiful eyes... Then both sides of your lips." They locked lips, tongues exploring gently. Their hands began wandering across each other's body, enjoying the familiarity beneath the clothes.

With a struggle, Dakota broke away, reaching in to his bag and pulling out a shiny maroon box. "Conor, we've been together for four years now."

"Four and a half," Conor interrupted, laughing as she sat up.

"Yes, well. I was going to wait until the right moment, and well, I wanted to ask..." Dakota got up onto one knee, holding the box out in front of him. "When I saw the star, I wished that I could spend the rest of our lives together. Conor Hagan, will you make my wish come true and marry me?"

Dakota saw a whole world inside her eyes as they glistened moistly. Conor blinked, smiling.

"Yes. Yes!" Conor said, smiling radiantly. "Yes, of course I will." She leaned forward and kissed Dakota again on the lips as he put the ring on her finger. They fell into the sand, laughing.

Conor held up her hand, admiring the sparkle of her ring in the moonlight.

"It's beautiful! You know me too well, Dakota. I love you."

"It was easy. I just found a diamond that resembled your eyes. I love you, too."

They lay in the sand holding hands, watching the sky and enjoying the serenity of the world around them. Conor was unable to resist the urge to admire the large diamond on her finger.

Suddenly, their laughter stopped. The sound of the rolling waves punctuated the streaks of fire in the sky, which grew into larger balls.

"What the Hell?" Dakota said, sitting up. Goose bumps formed on his skin. He wrenched his hand back towards him and pointed upwards. "They're some pretty big shooting stars!"

"I think we should go now," Conor said, standing up. She bent down for her sandals and bag, eyes glued to the skies above. Dakota stood beside her, his arm around her shoulders as they watched the sky light up. The world around them had become so bright that it almost seemed like daytime.

Although they had planned to leave, they remained rooted to the ground, unable to move as they stared at the night sky. They remained in place like statues, watching as flaming pebbles pummelled the ground around them.

Conor squealed as her hair began to smoulder, the acrid smell of burning hair mingling in their nostrils. It was like being caught in a burning hailstorm, the sky alight with precipitating fire.

The engaged couple began to run to their car, hands shielding their heads, the falling stars growing larger, until rocks the size of basketballs slammed into the ground, waves of sand flying through the smoky air. Conor tripped on a rock and fell to the ground, pulling Dakota with her. They lay in the sand, panting as they looked up at the flames falling towards them, the sound of their breaths dulled by the cacophony of crashing rocks.

"Still doubting the existence of a genie?" Conor asked. Dakota stared back at her, his lips tight together.

"Never mind," she said, shaking her head.

"I'm glad I get to spend the rest of my life with you," Dakota said, staring into Conor's watery eyes, watching as they reflected the blazing stars falling from the sky.

She grasped his hands in hers. "Me too. I love you, Dakota," she whispered.

"I love you, too, Conor," Dakota replied, before burning stars crushed their bodies into dust.

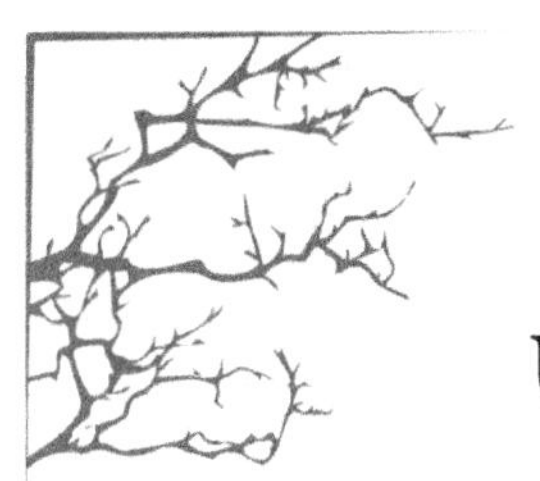

Up in the Air

K A-BOOM!

Another violent explosion shook the fragile surface below them. Everyone dropped to the ground and clung tightly to anything within reach. The fear of being shaken from the air overcoming all other senses. Eventually, the ruinous green clouds settled back into the infected surface from which they erupted. Slowly, everyone got up and went back to work.

"Why does that green cloud keep exploding, Mum?" Wirra asked, leaning over and pointing to the lurking green mist below him.

"Because, sweetheart, as time goes on it becomes more and more powerful, which causes it to explode more often," she replied, smiling. Wirra's eyes reflected the green tinge of the ground below, while her own were glassy with tears.

Wirra's mother remembered the year of 2034, one that brought humans face to face with an unimaginable disaster. It crept up on them like a cunning lion after its prey. Even when scientists warned of the approaching danger, humans ignorantly went about their daily lives in denial. They became used to the higher temperatures, the wilder weather. Politicians ignored the advice from scientists far more intelligent than themselves, promoting industry over the environment. In short, the politicians kept laws the same; pollution kept piling up in the environment around them. Homes were uprooted and families were viciously torn apart. People were not given enough time to prepare themselves for an uncontrollable event that would change their lives forever. For many, this wasn't long enough. Wirra and his mother only just made it out of the danger.

Scientists in first world countries had made huge replica cities on giant floating platforms. Huge engines worked tirelessly every day to keep the cities in the air, anchored at the core to the earth's surface. No safety fences were built around the edges; they just didn't have the time. Instead, Darwin's theory of evolution worked subconsciously in everyone's minds: survival of the fittest. If you fell, you died. Simple as that.

Soon after taking to the air, poisonous pollution condemned planet Earth and the living beings left behind, enveloping the surface completely with air the consistency of pea soup. Wirra loved the tales his mum would tell him about the old London days where people walked around in sludgy air which was so much like their own.

The day the floating cities were to be populated was one nobody would ever forget. Large crowds of families had flocked to the floating cities, eager to get their loved ones on-board, something Wirra's mother remembered all too well. It had been the most terrifying experience of her life. And the most distressing; she had had to leave large numbers of her family and friends behind in her attempt to get herself and Wirra to safety.

Even many of the families who made it to the gates weren't allowed on. There just simply wasn't enough space.

As the cities rose from the surface, screams of sheer terror filled the air. Families clung tightly to each other as they soared up into the unknown atmosphere. After floating upwards, the anchors proved their capabilities and slowly everyone began to calm down.

"If we never used bad fuels or smelly gases, would we still be down there?" Wirra asked as he looked over the edge. He wiped away the sheen of sweat on his face, pink-cheeked from the heat.

"Perhaps," his mother replied, feeling her own sweat glands working overtime to keep her cool.

"Do you think those anchors will hold forever?" Wirra asked as he surveyed the contraption below.

"Well, they have so far," his mother answered. Wirra was becoming increasingly excited.

"What if we could lower them and—"

"No, Wirra," his mother interrupted. "We are all staying here where it's safe."

Wirra frowned with disappointment and went back to looking at the world below him. He tried to make out shapes in the clouds, like he used to back on the surface. He imagined it to be a venomous snake, slithering its way around the surface and killing everything in its path.

Two months on the floating city seemed to be long enough for people to become familiar with the new way of life and start to move on from the terrifying disaster they had all experienced. Most people had shut the dangerous world below them out of their lives, trying to forget the past. They threw their energy towards keeping the city afloat. Tried to find ways of fixing the problems left behind on the surface. After all, they were still alive and needed to keep going. Billions of people had died in the poisonous gases below, left behind to suffocate in the fumes.

Wirra on the other hand, seemed fascinated by the glowing planet below him. He would spend hours each day lying in the lush green grass, peering over the edge. He never seemed to get bored and always looked as though he was expecting something amazing to happen.

Life on the floating platform wasn't much different to life on the surface. The adults worked on the engines, powered by solar nuclear technology; the children attended schools. There were no birds and no oceans, but the humans managed with what they had. Water was filtered from the atmosphere, kept in large reservoirs. There were no books, other than instruction manuals to run the engines. Food had been reduced to simple fruit and vegetables, and simple sources of protein, such as chickens, legumes, mushrooms, and insects. Bland, but palatable and sustaining.

"Can we ever go back home, Mum?" Wirra asked with curiosity, his eyes scanning the ruined world below.

"I don't think so, dear," his mother replied. "It's far too dangerous to return."

"But, what about—"

"No, Wirra," his mother cut in. "It's time to move on."

Earth looked like a spider with millions of legs. Anchors floated out in every direction to support the world's once-perfect cities. No one could be sure who made it out; travel was restricted to other floating cities on the basis of necessity. Only the leaders could travel, and they revealed nothing to the commoners. The communication engineers were working on re-establishing radio contact. Until that was open for public use, the citizens felt extremely lonely.

As Wirra lay on his belly, he scanned the world below. He was always looking out for something. He was the one who noticed when the lethal green clouds changed swirling direction last month, but it didn't seem to thrill him. He continued to do the same thing over and over again, like a determined scientist trying to prove a hypothesis.

"Come inside and get some lunch, Wirra, darling," his mother called from the house. With one last inspection of the polluted world below, Wirra stood up and made his way to the house for something to eat.

He would return to his grassy spot after lunch and continue to monitor the vicious clouds below. He would wait forever, if that's what it took him to find his little sister who was left behind. Maybe one day he would see her again. Until then, he would keep watching and waiting.

It's Going To Be You!

Dusk was long gone and the café was dimly lit and lonely. The street outside was quiet, except for a middle-aged man sitting near the door who trembled in his chair, looking nervously around the deserted street. He sat, licking his lips and jiggling his legs. He waited. Impatiently, but he waited.

Taking a sip of his fifth long black for the day, he saw the waiter approaching. The man stared into his eyes, like a predator hungry for the kill.

"You must be wired after all that coffee," the waiter said. His smile revealed his panic. No customer had ever stayed so long, except that author a while back, but she had been scribbling in a notebook as she watched the customers around her. "We're about to close, Sir, so I thought I'd ask if there was anything else you needed."

The man stared at the waiter, his gaze intense and burning. His fingers tapped a rhythm on his mug.

"Waiting for someone? Or..." The waiter trailed off, looking up and down the empty street. Shadows loomed among the buildings. During the day, workers and customers busily inhabited the street like ants. A constant rumble of white noise to infiltrate the day. But on this evening, all was quiet. The soft breeze was the only movement in the street.

"I'm waiting for my meal, actually," the man replied, his yellow teeth emerging behind tight lips.

The waiter's eyebrows raised. "Sorry, sir. I don't remember you ordering any food..." The waiter glanced inside the café.

"No, I didn't." The man reached into his bag beside him, bringing out a large kitchen knife. The blade glinted in the streetlight.

"I don't understand," the waiter mumbled, quivering. He took a step back.

"My meal," the man said, moving forward. "It's going to be you!"

A Pair of Socks – (A 100-word story)

The socks hung alone on the clothesline, swaying stiffly in the afternoon breeze. They were damp from the drizzle of rain earlier in the day, but the fierce sun had dried them again.

Below, the grass reached up, unmown and untidy. Within the jungle of grass a human body lay, bloated and peeling, its foetid stench unnoticed by any living thing.

The corpse's mouth opened, emitting a long guttural moan, joined by the hungry horde beyond the wooden fence. The zombie stood up, its head dragging the lifeless sock to the ground, before limping off in search of fresh meat.

Acknowledgements

Life threw a few hardballs at me while I wrote some of the stories for this anthology. My wife gave birth to our son, who was diagnosed with Hypoplastic Left Heart Syndrome. He had open-heart surgery only a week into his life, and spent the next few weeks recovering. We couldn't take him away from hospital until after his second surgery, five months later. In that time, normal life stood at a standstill while we spent each day just existing and doing what we needed to do to survive the ordeal.

Jonathan is doing as well as can be expected, but will need another major surgery to save his life in a few years.

I couldn't have possibly done any of it without the love and support of my wife, Jessica, our daughter, Liesel, and all our family and friends who helped us get by.

Thank you also to the huge team of medical staff at Buderim Private Hospital, Mater Hospital Brisbane, and Queensland Children's Hospital. Without you, we wouldn't have Jonathan in our lives.

The stories that hold this anthology together came from a variety of inspiration sources. Writing them helped me get through some hard days and took my mind to places darker than our reality. In doing this, it helped make the real world a less shitty place.

Some of these stories appeared first in other anthologies, and I'd like to thank the editors for their hard work collating them.

Atheria first appeared in Specul8 Publishing's dragon-themed anthology, *Hoards of the Great Fire Wyrms,* edited by TC Phillips.

Fire Escape first appeared in Dragon Faerie Creative Enterprise's charity anthology, *Challenge Accepted,* edited by Stephanie Barr.

Insomnia first appeared in Specul8 Publishing's demon-themed anthology, *Fire and Brimstone: A Demonic Compendium of the Wicked, Fallen and Accursed,* edited by TC Phillips.

If you've read this far, thank you. You're awesome. That's why you're my favourite. Don't tell the others; it'll be our little secret.

I hope you enjoyed reading *Shadows In The Flames*. I would love if you could share your thoughts as a review on your favourite sales platform or Goodreads, even if they are just a few words and a star rating. Every review helps new readers find my work.

Please feel free to chat with me on social media. I love to connect with my readers; you can find me on Facebook, Instagram, WordPress or Twitter, where you will find news on upcoming stories and releases.

Until next time.

Don't miss out!

Visit the website below and you can sign up to receive emails whenever Scott G. Gibson publishes a new book. There's no charge and no obligation.

https://books2read.com/r/B-A-FAYB-GMVU

BOOKS 2 READ

Connecting independent readers to independent writers.

Did you love *Shadows In the Flames*? Then you should read *Shadows of a Nightmare*[1] by Scott G. Gibson!

[2]

Shadows of a Nightmare is a short story collection to haunt your nightmares and end the world as you know it.

These chilling tales are not ashamed of splashing blood across the page and crawling into the shadowy depths of horror: "The Rage", a grisly apocalyptic tale where a viral plague of anger overcomes humans; "Meat Market", about a killer monster who preys on gym-junkies to eat their well-toned flesh; "The Ghost", a harrowing supernatural tale about a man who is haunted by the world's most murderous spirit; "Alien Invasion", a story of extra-terrestrial beings

---

1. https://books2read.com/u/4EDeqz

2. https://books2read.com/u/4EDeqz

taking over the world; "The Man in the Van" shows us what happens when an amateur sleuth tries to save his girlfriend from a vicious kidnapper; "Such is Life" asks what would happen if somebody went back in time to stop Ned Kelly and his gang from being killed at Glenrowan; plus many more.

Are you ready to enter a labyrinth of fear and thrills? Scott G Gibson's *Shadows of a Nightmare* brings you spine-tingling stories to keep you awake at night. Read them if you dare.

Read more at https://scottggibson.wordpress.com/.

Also by Scott G. Gibson

Bad Luck Bevin
Bad Luck Bevin

Shadows
Shadows of a Nightmare
Shadows In the Flames

Standalone
Place Your Hand in Mine
Making Tracks

About the Author

Scott G. Gibson is an independent author and high school teacher living in Queensland with his wife, Jess, and children, Liesel and Jonathan. In his limited spare time he enjoys reading, playing chess, and sharing puns of debatable quality.

Read more at https://scottggibson.wordpress.com/.